Get a Feel for English !

喚醒你的英文語感 ！

Get a Feel for English!

喚醒你的英文語感！

神明護體學英文
日常英語篇

總編審：王復國
作者：吉田研作、荒井貴和、武藤克彥
「完全改訂版　起きてから寝るまで英語表現700」

Preface

● 利用本書的句型結構來培養更好的傳達力及表現力

　　本書的基本概念為：以<u>一個人就能進行英語會話</u>的想法為基礎，將我們平日所想到的、所感覺到的一切都化為言語，用自言自語的方式來練習。而只要能靈活運用以下四大領域之表達方式，你就一定能充分說明日常生活中的一切。

　　1）行為表現（I make breakfast.）

　　2）說明既有狀態（The weather doesn't look too good.）

　　3）心情（I feel terrible when I skip breakfast.）

　　4）感受與想法（Should I take my umbrella to work today?）

　　若能充分表達行為、狀態說明、心情、想法感受這 4 大領域，你的英語口說基礎能力就算是相當好了。但由於本書所列例句都是以多數人的共通日常生活經驗為基準來挑選，不見得能涵蓋每個人的實際經驗。故重要的是，讀者應將本書介紹的句型結構做為個人經驗的參考。例如，上述的 I make breakfast. 若改為「煮咖啡」，就是 I make coffee.，而喝味增湯的人則可改成 I make miso soup.。The weather doesn't look too good. 適用於天氣不好的時候；若碰上好天氣，就改成 The weather looks good.；若碰上塞車，則可說 The traffic doesn't look good.。另外，I feel terrible when I skip breakfast. 這句若應用在宿醉方面，便可說成 I feel terrible when I have too much to drink.；反之，若欲表達早睡的話感覺會很舒服，就改為 I feel great when I go to bed early.。最後，像 Should I take my umbrella to work today? 這種用於猶豫不決時的句型，也可應用在因時間不夠而猶豫是否該搭計程車的情況，亦即可改成 Should I take the taxi?。

　　本書中的各種句型是由法國學者弗朗索瓦‧古茵（Francois Gouin）於 19 世紀所開發之教學方法發展而來，透過以英語表達自身行為、情緒、想法等的方式，達成提升英語傳達力及表現力之目的。

　　請參考本書，試著以英語盡情表達自己的一切吧！

　　　　　　　　　　上智大學外語學院英語系教授　吉田研作

Contents
目錄

前言 　　　　　　　　　　　P.2
本書結構與使用方法 　　　　P.6

chapter **1** 早 晨 In the Morning
單字篇／身體動作／自言自語／Skit ／ Quick Check 　　P.11

chapter **2** 通 勤 Commuting
單字篇／身體動作／自言自語／Skit ／ Quick Check 　　P.39

chapter **3** 家 事 Housework
單字篇／身體動作／自言自語／Skit ／ Quick Check 　　P.63

chapter **4** 辦公室工作 Working at the Office
單字篇／身體動作／自言自語／Skit ／ Quick Check 　　P.93

chapter **5** 資訊生活 The IT Life
單字篇／身體動作／自言自語／Skit ／ Quick Check
與部落格有關的句型 　　P.119

chapter 6 在家放鬆 Relaxing at Home
單字篇／身體動作／自言自語／Skit／Quick Check **P.149**

chapter 7 假日外出 Going Out on a Day Off
單字篇／身體動作／自言自語／Skit／Quick Check **P.167**

chapter 8 外 食 Eating Out
單字篇／身體動作／自言自語／Skit／Quick Check **P.193**

chapter 9 健康與飲食 Health & Diet
單字篇／身體動作／自言自語／Skit／Quick Check **P.223**

chapter 10 夜晚 At Night
單字篇／身體動作／自言自語／Skit／Quick Check **P.249**

Column
1. 利用電影或電視影集，製作專屬於你的原創句型集 **P.201**
2. 練習運用例句來讓會話更順暢 **P.257**

本書結構與使用方法
How to Use This Book

本書整體結構與使用方法

■將一整天從早到晚的一般生活場景分成十章。

■各章又再分成「單字篇」、「身體動作」、「自言自語」、「Skit（對話）」、「Quick Check（測驗）」等部分。

■讀者可從自己較有興趣、與自身狀況類似，或與自己目前所在地點較接近的場景開始閱讀。

■只要反覆進行「自言自語的練習」，讓自己能以英語陳述周遭一切事物，就能順利提升自己的英語口說能力了。

各章結構與使用方法

〔單字篇〕

■在此會將各場景中，各種周遭事物的單字和對應的插圖一同搭配呈現。而這些單字幾乎都會出現在後續「身體動作」和「自言自語」部分的例句或說明中。

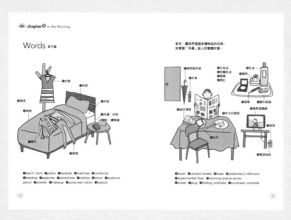

※首先，請試著將插圖內的中文翻譯成英文，解答就在下方。透過此單字篇，你便能對該章產生一個概略的印象，也就等於是在全力學習各種英語表達方式前，先做個暖身運動。

〔身體動作篇〕

■列出各場景中常進行之行為、動作的英語敘述，也就是，將外在行動轉化為語言敘述。這類句子通常看似簡單，但要用英語講時，卻又經常卡住、一時說不出口。請一一聽取，並不斷反覆練習說出這些你每天都會進行的動作，直到徹底記住為止。

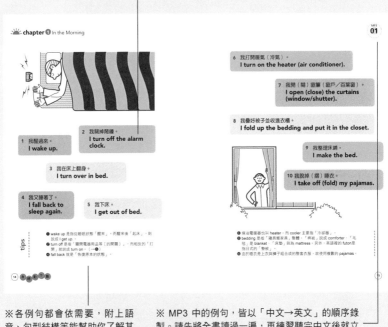

MP3
01

6 我打開暖氣（冷氣）。
I turn on the heater (air conditioner).

7 我開（關）窗簾（窗戶／百葉窗）。
I open (close) the curtains (window/shutter).

8 我疊好被子並收進衣櫃。
I fold up the bedding and put it in the closet.

1 我醒過來。
I wake up.

2 我關掉鬧鐘。
I turn off the alarm clock.

9 我整理床鋪。
I make the bed.

3 我在床上翻身。
I turn over in bed.

10 我脫掉（摺）睡衣。
I take off (fold) my pajamas.

4 我又睡著了。
I fall back to sleep again.

5 我下床。
I get out of bed.

tips
● wake up 是指仍處睡眠狀態「醒來」。而醒來後「起床」，則說成 I get up。
● turn off 是指「關閉電器用品等（的開關）」，而相反的「打開」，就說成 turn on。（一）
● fall back 是指「恢復原本的狀態」。

● 保冷電暖器也叫 heater。而 cooler 主要指「冷卻器」。
● bedding 是「寢具類家具」，整體、「棉被」，說成 comforter。「毛毯」是 blanket。「床墊」則為 mattress。另外，英語裡的 futon 是指日式的「墊被」。
● 由於睡衣是上衣與褲子組合成的整套衣服，故使用複數的 pajamas。

14 晨起篇　身體動作

15

※各例句都會依需要，附上語意、句型結構等能幫助你了解其表達方式的說明。

※ MP3 中的例句，皆以「中文→英文」的順序錄製。請先將全書讀過一遍，再練習聽完中文後就立即說出英文來。

怎樣才能將句型記得更牢？

請利用 MP3 中所收錄的例句或對話來進行「跟讀練習」。所謂的「跟讀練習」就是一邊聽，一邊將所聽到的句子立即覆誦出來。越是將發音、節奏、語調模仿得維妙維肖，效果就越理想。一開始也許很難跟上 MP3 的速度，但是只要不斷反覆練習，就一定能說得流利。而屆時，不論是單字還是句型，都將成為你的一部分，徹底烙印在你的腦海中。

〔自言自語篇〕

■本篇處理的是心裡或腦中的「內在」世界，也就是，列出大腦或心裡所想事情的各種表達方式。而這類「將以自己為中心的內在世界言語化」，即「自言自語」的表達方式，其實比千篇一律的會話句型要豐富、有趣得多。

※雖然「自言自語」部分也納入了許多可應用在會話中、能表達自身情緒的實用說法，不過一開始還是以自言自語的方式練習較好。

※MP3 中的例句皆以「中文→英文」的順序錄製。請先將全書讀過一遍，再練習聽完中文後就立即說出英文來。

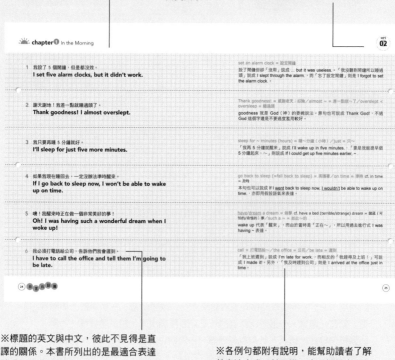

※標題的英文與中文，彼此不見得是直譯的關係。本書所列出的是最適合表達該感覺的道地英語。

※各例句都附有說明，能幫助讀者了解其表達方式，甚至進一步理解語意和句型結構，並學到更進階的單字及說法。

〔Skit 對話〕

■在此提供彙集了各章句型而成的會話形式，以協助讀者將已學到之表達方式應用於實際對話中。請將此部分視為活用所學句型之實踐單元，並把自己當成會話主角來反覆練習。

※曾出現在「身體動作」、「自言自語」等部份的表達方式，會以褐色標出。

〔Quick Check 小測驗〕

這裡的題目以出現於各章但並未出現於 Skit 部分的句型為主。請依據中文的意思，來完成對應的英文句子。若碰到不懂的句型，就隨時翻回對應頁面去複習。

〔本書的各種標記說明〕

在本書中，除了特別標註的部分外，都以美式英語之標記、發音為準。各種標記符號的說明如下：

cf.	請參考比較以下資訊
e.g.	以下為舉例
____/____	斜線前後有底線的部分可相互替換，意思不變
[ ]	可加上 [ ] 內的單字、片語
( )	可替換為 ( ) 中的單字、片語（但意思會改變）
< >	< > 內為情況說明
-ing	指動詞加ing

chapter 1　In the Morning ☀

早晨

早晨總是忙碌的。
爬出被窩、梳洗更衣，吃早餐……
要打理的事好多，
從一天的開始，腦袋就忙得停不下來了。

Words 單字篇

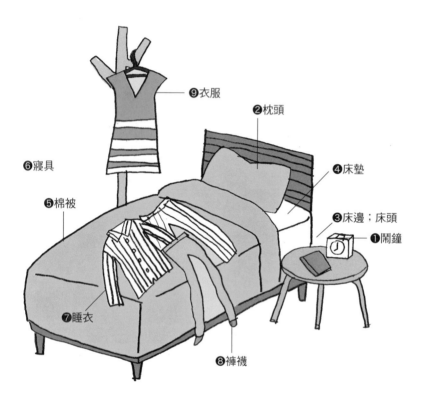

❾衣服
❷枕頭
❹床墊
❻寢具
❺棉被
❸床邊；床頭
❶鬧鐘
❼睡衣
❽褲襪

❶alarm clock ❷pillow ❸bedside ❹mattress ❺comforter
❻bedding ❼pajamas ❽pantyhose ❾clothes ❿lotion ⓫eyebrow
pencil ⓬powder ⓭makeup ⓮sunscreen lotion ⓯lipstick

首先，讓我們透過各種物品的名稱，
來掌握「早晨」給人的整體印象。

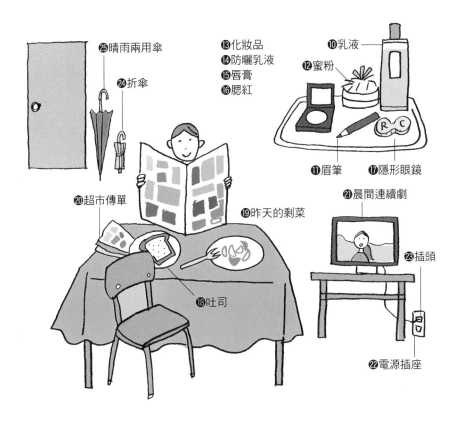

㉕晴雨兩用傘

㉔折傘

⑬化妝品
⑭防曬乳液
⑮唇膏
⑯腮紅

⑩乳液

⑫蜜粉

⑪眉筆　　⑰隱形眼鏡

㉑晨間連續劇

⑳超市傳單

⑲昨天的剩菜

㉓插頭

⑱吐司

㉒電源插座

⑯blush　⑰contact lenses　⑱toast　⑲yesterday's leftovers
⑳supermarket flyer　㉑morning drama series
㉒outlet　㉓plug　㉔folding umbrella　㉕sunshade umbrella

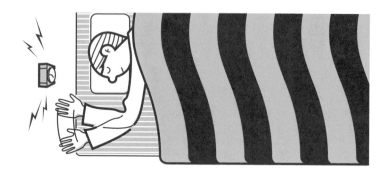

2　我關掉鬧鐘。
I turn off the alarm clock.

1　我醒過來。
I wake up.

3　我在床上翻身。
I turn over in bed.

4　我又睡著了。
I fall back to sleep again.

5　我下床。
I get out of bed.

tips

❶ wake up 是指從睡眠狀態「醒來」。而醒來後「起床」，則說成 I get up.。
❷ turn off 是指「關閉電器用品等〔的開關〕」，而相反的「打開」就說成 turn on。（→❻）
❹ fall back 就是「恢復原本的狀態」。

6 我打開暖氣（冷氣）。
I turn on the heater (air conditioner).

7 我開（關）窗簾（窗戶／百葉窗）。
I open (close) the curtains (window/shutter).

8 我疊好被子並收進衣櫃。
I fold up the bedding and put it in the closet.

9 我整理床鋪。
I make the bed.

10 我脫掉（摺）睡衣。
I take off (fold) my pajamas.

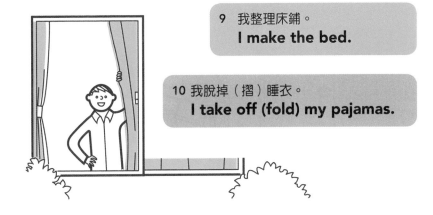

❻ 煤油電暖器也叫 heater。而 cooler 主要指「冷卻器」。

❽ bedding 是指「寢具類家具」整體。「棉被」說成 comforter、「毛毯」是 blanket、「床墊」則為 mattress。另外，英語裡的 futon 是指日式的「墊被」。

❿ 由於睡衣是上衣與褲子組合成的整套衣服，故使用複數的 pajamas。

11 我去上廁所。
I go to the bathroom.

12 我沖馬桶。
I flush the toilet.

13 我洗手。
I wash my hands.

14 我擦手。
I dry my hands.

15 我開（關）水龍頭。
I turn the faucet on (off).

tips

❶ bathroom 是「浴室」也是「廁所」，go to the bathroom 則為「上廁所」之意。

❷ flush 是指「用水沖洗」。

❸ 「洗手」通常都用兩隻手，故使用複數的 hands。

❹ 「用毛巾擦臉」說成 wipe one's face with a towel。

16 我刷牙。
I brush my teeth.

17 我漱口。
I rinse out my mouth.

18 我仰頭漱口。
I gargle.

19 我搶著先用洗手台。
I fight over using the wash basin first.

20 我淋浴。
I take a shower.

⓯ 供水的「水龍頭」也可說成 tap，而開、關水龍頭就用 turn on/off。
另外「開（關）水」說成 turn on (off) the water。「扭開水龍頭」則
說成 run a faucet。

⓳ fight over~ 就是「爭奪～」。「浴室洗臉台」叫 bathroom vanity，
而「盥洗用具」用複數的 toiletries 來表示。

21 我刮鬍子。
I shave.

22 我擤鼻涕。
I blow my nose.

23 我擦一些乳液。
I put on some lotion.

24 我把亂髮梳整齊。
I smooth down my messy hair.

25 我整理頭髮。
I do my hair.

tips

㉓ 「化妝」說成 <u>put on</u> / <u>wear</u> makeup;「底妝」為 makeup base;「防曬乳液」是 <u>sun block</u> / <u>sunscreen lotion</u>;「蜜粉」則叫 powder;「腮紅」為 blush;而「唇膏／口紅」則為 lipstick。

㉔ messy 是指頭髮「散亂不整齊」的樣子。

㉕ 「整理頭髮」也可說成 fix one's hairdo。「梳頭髮」說成 <u>brush</u> / <u>comb</u> one's hair,「吹乾頭髮」則是 blow-dry one's hair。

26 我依據今天的行程來選衣服。
I choose my clothes according to my schedule.

27 我穿上襯衫（長褲／裙子）。
I put on my shirt (pants/skirt).

28 我替小孩穿衣服。
I dress my child.

29 我去拿報紙。
I go get the newspaper.

30 我澆花。
I water the flowers.

㉖「依據行程」也可說成 based on my plans。
㉗ 穿戴在身上的東西，如hat（帽子）、shoes（鞋子）、glasses（眼鏡）、contact lenses（隱形眼鏡）、watch（手錶）等，也都可使用 put on。
㉘ 這裡的 dress 為及物動詞，表示「替～穿衣服」之意。

31 我燒開一些水。
I boil some water.

32 我泡咖啡。
I make coffee.

33 我烤吐司。
I make toast.

34 我把牛奶從冰箱裡拿出來。
I get the milk out of the refrigerator.

35 我打開收音機（電視）。
I turn on the radio (TV).

tips

㉜ 「泡咖啡」也可說成 brew coffee，而「倒在杯子裡」則說成
pour some coffee in <u>a</u> / <u>the</u> cup。
㉝ 「烤些麵包」可說成 toast some bread。
㉞ 「冰箱」在會話中經常被簡稱為 fridge。
㉟ 「連續劇」也可說成 serial drama。

36 我收聽〔廣播的〕外語教學課程。
I listen to a foreign language course [on the radio].

37 我看晨間連續劇。
I watch a morning drama series.

38 我看電視上的運勢分析。
I check my fortune on TV.

39 我設定〔錄放影機的〕預約錄影來錄電視節目。
I set the [VCR] timer to record a TV program.

40 我查看一下超市傳單。
I check the supermarket flyers.

❸❽ fortune 是指「運勢」;「算命」叫 fortune-telling;而「看氣象預報（交通資訊）」則說成 check the weather (traffic) report on TV.

❸❾ VCR 為 videocassette recorder 的縮寫,就是指「錄放影機」。

❹⓿ flyer（傳單）也可拼成 flier。

41 我餵貓（狗）
I feed the cat (dog).

42 我去遛狗。
I take my dog for a walk.

43 我關（開）燈。
I switch off (on) the light.

44 我拔掉電線的插頭。
I unplug the cord.

45 我關門並上鎖。
I close the door and lock it.

tips

❹❶ feed 是「餵～飼料」之意，而「飼料」就是 food。
❹❷ take ～ for a walk 是指「帶～去散步」。
❹❸ 「關（開）」也可用 turn off (on)。（→❷）
❹❹ 在牆壁上的電源插座（插孔）叫 outlet，而接在電器用品上的插頭叫 plug。

46 我檢查門鎖。
I check the lock.

47 我開車載先生（孩子）去車站。
I give my husband (child) a ride to the station.

㊻ 「我檢查門是否有鎖好」可説成 I make sure the door is locked.
㊼ 「開車把人送到～」也可用 drive（人）to ～ 的講法。若是「走路送人去」的話，則用 walk（人）to ～。至於「送別某人」則是 see（人）off。

1　我設了 5 個鬧鐘，但是都沒效。
I set five alarm clocks, but it didn't work.

2　謝天謝地！我差一點就睡過頭了。
Thank goodness! I almost overslept.

3　我只要再睡 5 分鐘就好。
I'll sleep for just five more minutes.

4　如果我現在睡回去，一定沒辦法準時醒來。
If I go back to sleep now, I won't be able to wake up on time.

5　噢！我醒來時正在做一個非常美好的夢！
Oh! I was having such a wonderful dream when I woke up!

6　我必須打電話給公司，告訴他們我會遲到。
I have to call the office and tell them I'm going to be late.

set an alarm clock = 設定鬧鐘

設了鬧鐘但卻「沒用」說成 ... but it was useless.。「我沒聽到鬧鐘所以睡過頭」說成 I slept through the alarm.，而「忘了設定鬧鐘」則是 I forgot to set the alarm clock.。

Thank goodness! = 感謝老天；好險／almost ~ = 差一點就~了／overslept < oversleep = 睡過頭

goodness 就是 God（神）的委婉說法。原句也可說成 Thank God!，不過 God 這個字還是不要過度濫用較好。

---

sleep for ~ minutes (hours) = 睡~分鐘（小時）／just = 只~

「我再 5 分鐘就醒來」說成 I'll wake up in five minutes.，「要是我能提早個 5 分鐘起床，~」則說成 If I could get up five minutes earlier, ~ .

---

go back to sleep (=fall back to sleep) = 再睡著／on time = 準時 cf. in time = 及時

本句也可以說成 If I went back to sleep now, I wouldn't be able to wake up on time.，亦即用假設語氣來表達。

---

have/dream a dream = 做夢 cf. have a bad (terrible/strange) dream = 做惡（可怕的/奇怪的）夢／such a ~ = 如此~的

wake up 代表「醒來」，而由於當時是「正在~」，所以用過去進行式 I was having ~ 表達。

---

call = 打電話給~／the office = 公司／be late = 遲到

「我上班遲到」說成 I'm late for work.，而相反的「我趕得及上班！」可說成 I made it!。另外，「我及時趕到公司」則是 I arrived at the office just in time。

7 ＜對於怎麼叫都叫不起來的家人＞〔上班（上學）〕遲到了可別怪我。

<To a family member who won't wake up> Don't blame me if you are late [for work (school)].

8 陰天時我會覺得情緒低落。

I feel down when it's cloudy.

9 我宿醉很嚴重。

I have a terrible hangover.

10 我昨晚送出的電子郵件還沒收到回覆。

I didn't get a reply to the e-mail I sent last night.

11 呃，我喉嚨痛。我想我是感冒了。

Ugh, my throat feels sore. I think I've caught a cold.

12 ＜在冬天＞早上變得越來越難從床上爬起來。

<In the winter> It's getting harder to get out of bed in the morning.

blame = 責怪〜 e.g. Don't blame me if 〜 .= 要是〜可別怪我

這句也可說成「遲到了可不關我的事！」It's none of my business if you are late!，而「你為什麼不叫醒我？」說成 Why didn't you wake me up?。

---

feel down (= feel low) = 情緒低落 cf. feel gloomy = 感覺憂鬱／cloudy = 多雲的

「正在下雨」說成 it's raining.。而相反的「天氣一好心情也跟著變好」則可說成 I feel uplifted/cheerful when it's clear and sunny.

---

terrible = 嚴重的；糟糕的／hangover = 宿醉

「我昨晚喝太多了」說成 I drank too much last night.。「酒醉」叫 drunk，而「〔爛醉（醉得不省人事）〕」則是 get [very (hopelessly)] drunk。

---

reply = 回覆；回信

「我沒收到回覆」也可說成 I got no reply.，「收到電子郵件」說成 get / receive an e-mail，而想說「寄電子郵件給我吧」就用 E-mail me. / Send me an e-mail. 即可。

Ugh =呃／sore = 疼痛 e.g. I have a sore throat. = 我喉嚨痛。／caught a cold < catch a cold = 感冒

「我喉嚨癢癢的」說成 My throat feels itchy.；「〔打〕噴嚏」叫 sneeze；「流鼻水」是 have a runny nose；而「鼻塞」則是 have a stuffy nose。

---

get hard = 變得困難／get out of bed = 從床上爬起來

get out of bed 也可改為 get up。若要說明理由，就在後面加上 because it's getting colder（因為天氣越來越冷）之類的即可。

13 我無法決定該穿什麼！
I can't decide what to wear!

14 也許我可以穿前幾天剛買的新衣服。
Maybe I can wear those brand-new clothes that I bought the other day.

15 我今天要和客戶開會，所以必須穿得整齊點。
I have a meeting with some clients today, so I have to dress neatly.

16 我今天的髮型不太理想。
My hair doesn't look very nice today.

17 我匆匆忙忙地穿上絲襪，結果絲襪就脫線了。
I put on a pair of stockings in a hurry and made a run in them.

18 我領帶打不好。
I can't tie my necktie neatly.

decide ＝ 決定／what to ～ ＝ 該做～

「我該穿什麼？」說成 What should I wear?；「我挑選明天要穿的衣服」說成 I pick out my clothes for tomorrow.；而「我找不出其他可穿的衣服！」則是 I can't find anything else to wear!。

---

maybe ～ ＝ 也許／brand-new ＝ 全新的／bought<buy ＝ 買／the other day ＝ 前幾天；之前

你也可以具體說出要穿的衣服，例如「這件全新的連身裙（西裝／外套／襯衫）」this brand-new dress (suit/jacket/shirt)。

---

client ＝ 顧客；客戶／dress ＝ 穿衣服／neatly ＝ 整齊地

也可用 dress properly（穿適當的衣服）。「穿西裝打領帶」說成 wear a suit and tie；「盛裝打扮」說成 get all dressed up；而「穿得隨興」則是 dress casually。

---

my hair ＝ 我的頭髮〔髮型〕／look nice (= look good) ＝ 看起來很好

「整理頭髮」說成 do / fix one's hair。另外，good hair day（頭髮很理想的日子）有「一切順利的日子」之意。

---

stockings ＝ 絲襪 cf. pantyhose ＝ 褲襪／in a hurry ＝ 匆忙地／run ＝ 脫線

注意，絲襪是成對的，所以要用複數型。a pair of ～「一雙～」，而此例句也可改為 There is a run in my stockings because I put them on in such a rush.。

---

tie ＝ 打（結）；繫／necktie ＝ 領帶（較常說成 tie）／neatly ＝ 整齊地 cf. nicely ＝ 好好地；漂亮地

「打」領帶說成 put on / wear a tie；「拉直領帶」說成 straighten one's tie；「鬆開領帶」是 loosen up one's tie；而「拿掉領帶」則是 take off one's tie。

19 我今早的妝上得很好。
The makeup is going on my face really well this morning.

20 哎呀，我今天怎樣就是畫不好眉毛！
Gee, I just can't get this eyebrow pencil right today!

21 我的隱形眼鏡一直戴不上去。
I'm having trouble putting in my contact lenses.

22 水已經涼掉了（變溫了）。
The water has gotten cold (warm).

23 我一定不能忘記要防範花粉症。
I mustn't forget to guard against hay fever.

24 我吃昨天的剩菜當早餐就好。
I'll just have yesterday's leftovers for breakfast.

makeup = 化妝（品）／go = 呈現

「化妝」是 <u>wear</u> / <u>put on</u> makeup；「補妝」則是 fix makeup；而「畫淡妝」可說成 wear a touch of makeup。

Gee為感嘆詞。eyebrow pencil = 眉筆／eyebrow = 眉毛 cf. eyelashes = 睫毛

「畫眉毛」也可說成 pencil in one's eyebrows，而「用眉筆」則說成 use an eyebrow pencil。

---

have trouble -ing = 做～時遇到困難／contact lens = 隱形眼鏡（複數為 lenses。也可簡稱為 contact[s]）

「戴（拿下）隱形眼鏡」說成 put on (take out) one's contact lenses，而「戴著隱形眼鏡」為 wear <u>contacts</u> / <u>contact lenses</u>。

---

has gotten cold 為完成式，表示「水變涼了」的狀態。若是「水漸漸變涼（變溫）」，就用進行式 The water is getting cold (warm).，而「空氣漸漸變冷（變暖）」則說成 The air is getting cold (warm).。

---

guard against ~ = 小心防備～ cf. take precautions against ~ = 針對～採取預防措施／hay fever (= pollen allergy) = 花粉症；花粉過敏

「花粉症的季節」叫 hay fever season。「我有花粉症」說成 I have hay fever.，而「我為花粉症所苦」則說成 I suffer from hay fever.。

---

leftovers = 剩下的〔飯菜〕（通常用複數）／have ~ for breakfast = 吃～當作早餐

「熱剩菜」說成 heat leftovers；「把剩菜收進冰箱」說成 put the leftovers in the refrigerator；而「用剩菜做點吃的」則可說 make something with the leftovers。

25 如果不吃早餐我會很不舒服。
I feel terrible when I skip breakfast.

26 我把吐司烤焦了！
I burned the toast!

27 今天沒報紙嗎？
Aren't there any newspapers today?

28 ＜電視上的運勢資訊＞太好了！今天金牛座（我的星座）運勢最佳！
<On TV fortune-telling> Lucky me! Taurus (My sign) is the luckiest star sign today!

29 不知道今天的氣象預報準不準。
I wonder if the weather forecast is accurate today.

30 我該帶把摺疊傘嗎？
Should I bring a folding umbrella?

feel terrible = 感覺很糟 cf. feel bad = 感覺不舒服／skip = 省略～

「吃早餐」説成 <u>have</u> / <u>eat</u> breakfast，而「沒吃早餐就去上班」則是 go to work without breakfast。

---

burn = 把～燒焦／toast = 吐司麵包 cf. 做為動詞則表示「烤；烘」之意。

「烤吐司」可説成 make <u>toast</u> / <u>toast bread</u>。（注意make a toast 是指「敬酒」。）「一片吐司」是 a <u>piece</u> / <u>slice</u> of toast，而「在吐司上抹奶油」則説成 <u>butter toast</u> / <u>spread butter on toast</u>。

---

newspaper (= paper) = 報紙

「送報」是 deliver newspapers，而「訂報紙」是 take a newspaper。另外，「停刊日」翻成英文是 newspaper holiday，但是一般不太使用這種説法。

Lucky me! = 我走運了！ cf. Lucky you! =你真幸運！／Taurus = 金牛座

「占星術」是 <u>horoscope</u> / <u>astrology</u>，「星座」則為 [star] sign。「相信星座運勢／算命」就説成 believe in <u>horoscopes</u> / <u>fortune-telling</u>。

I wonder if ～ = 我懷疑～是否～／weather forecast = 氣象預報／accurate = 正確的；準確的

本句也可改用 prove right（説中；説對）來表達，説成 Will the forecast prove right today? 而「氣象預報準確（不準）」可説成 The weather forecast was right (wrong).。

---

bring = 帶～／folding = 折疊式的／umbrella = 傘 cf. parasol = 陽傘 /sunshade umbrella = 晴雨兩用傘

「撐（開）傘」説成 <u>open</u> / <u>put up</u> an umbrella，「收傘」則是 <u>close</u> / <u>fold</u> an umbrella。

31 我今天要搭比平常早一班的車。
I'll take an earlier train than usual today.

---

32 這電視節目實在太有趣了，讓我沒辦法出門。
This TV program is so amusing that I cannot leave home.

---

earlier =（時間上）在前面的；較早的 cf. earlier than usual = 比平常早／take a train = 搭火車 cf. take the subway (bus) = 搭地鐵（巴士）

用 catch the train 可表達「趕火車」之意，而「錯過〔平常坐的〕車班」則説成 miss one's [usual] train。

---

so ～ that ... = 如此～以至於⋯／amusing = 有趣的；好玩的 cf. funny = 滑稽的；好笑的

「節目實在太有趣，讓我無法出門」也可説成 I can't go out because this program is so funny.。另外因「看電視看得入迷而緊盯著電視」則可説成 I'm glued to the TV.。

Skit  早晨篇

忙碌老媽與厚臉皮兒子之 「缺乏倫理的早晨」

Son: **Mom, hurry up❶. I have to eat breakfast. I feel terrible
when I skip breakfast.**

Mom: **Make yourself some toast. I'm having trouble putting in
my contact lenses.**

S: **I don't want toast today.**

M: **Then just have yesterday's leftovers for breakfast. You can
microwave❷ the spaghetti.**

S: **Spaghetti for breakfast! Are you crazy, Mom?**

M: **Then have some cereal❸. Gee❹, I just can't seem to get this
eyebrow pencil right today.**

S: **There is a run❺ in your stockings.**

M: **Damn❻. I put them on in a rush❼. I'll wear the new pants I
bought the other day. Then I won't need the stockings.**

S: **Fine. Just do it quickly.**

M: **Oh, I still have to brush my teeth and make my bed.**

S: **Nobody cares❽ if you don't make your bed.**

M: **All right. Give me five more minutes and then I'll drive you
to the station.**

S: **Hurry up, Mom! And don't blame me if you're late for work!**

兒子：媽，快點！我必須吃早餐。不吃早餐我就不舒服。

媽媽：自己去烤些吐司。我的隱形眼鏡一直戴不上去。

兒子：我今天不想吃吐司。

媽媽：那就吃昨天的剩菜當早餐。你可以用微波爐把義大利麵加熱。

兒子：早餐吃義大利麵？媽，你瘋了嗎？

媽媽：那就吃點早餐穀片。唉呀，我今天怎樣就是畫不好眉毛！

兒子：妳的絲襪脫線了。

媽媽：真該死！我穿得太匆忙了。我還是穿前幾天買的新褲子好了。這樣
　　　就不需要絲襪了。

兒子：好啊，總之快點兒就是了。

媽媽：噢，我還得刷牙跟整理床鋪。

兒子：床鋪不整理沒人會在意啦。

媽媽：好啦。再等我 5 分鐘，我就開車送你去車站。

兒子：媽，趕快！妳要是上班遲到了可別怪到我頭上！

【單字片語】

❶ hurry up：趕快；快點兒

❷ microwave：用微波爐加熱

❸ cereal：早餐穀片（玉米片或燕麥片
　　等）

❹ Gee：哎呀（表示失望或焦慮不滿的感
　　嘆詞）

❺ run：（絲襪等東西的）脫線

❻ Damn.：可惡；該死（口語）

❼ in a rush：匆匆地

❽ care：在意；在乎

Quick Check

讓我們一起來複習本章所介紹過的句型！請依據以下中文句子的意思，來完成對應的英文句子。（答案就在本頁最下方。）

❶ 我又睡著了。 →P014

I ( ) ( ) to ( ) again.

❷ 我疊好被子並收進衣櫃。 →P015

I ( ) ( ) the ( ) and ( ) it ( ) the ( ).

❸ 我漱口。 →P017

I ( ) ( ) my ( ).

❹ 我把亂髮梳整齊。 →P018

I ( ) ( ) my ( ) hair.

❺ 我拔掉電線的插頭。 →P022

I ( ) the ( ).

❻ 謝天謝地！我差一點就睡過頭了。 →P024

( ) ( )! I almost ( ).

❼ 〈對於怎麼叫都叫不起來的家人〉上學遲到了可別怪我。 →P026

( ) ( ) me ( ) you are late for school.

❽ 呃，我喉嚨痛。我想我是感冒了。 →P026

Ugh, my ( ) ( ) ( ). I think I've ( ) a ( ).

❾ 我今早的妝上得很好。 →P030

The ( ) is ( ) ( ) my face really ( ) this morning.

❿ 不知道今天的氣象預報準不準。 →P032

I ( ) ( ) the ( ) ( ) is ( ) today.

---

❶ fall/back/sleep ❷ fold/up/bedding/put/in/ closet ❸ rinse/out/mouth ❹ smooth/down/ messy ❺ unplug/cord ❻ Thank/goodness/ overslept ❼ Don't/blame/if ❽ throat/feels/ sore/caught/cold ❾ makeup/going/on/well ❿ wonder/if/weather/forecast/accurate

chapter 2 Commuting

通勤

本章以火車通勤為例進行練習。
列車進站後，等待的人們魚貫上車，
陌生人們一同乘車前往各自的目的地⋯⋯
在這樣的過程中，
往往能看見不少人間縮影，
於是內心的呢喃就更多了。

Words 單字篇

❻驗票口

❷號誌燈（紅綠燈）

❼儲值火車票卡

❸行人

❶行人穿越道

❹地下道
❺車站

❽列車；火車　⓬乘客

⓮普通車
⓯平快車
⓰快車
⓱特快車
⓲女性專用車廂

❾排隊隊伍　❿乘車位置　⓫月台　⓬乘客　⓭站務人員

❶ crosswalk ❷ light ❸ pedestrian ❹ underpass ❺ station ❻ ticket gate ❼ prepaid railway pass ❽ train ❾ line ❿ boarding point ⓫ platform ⓬ passenger ⓭ station employee ⓮ local train

首先，讓我們透過各種物品的名稱，來掌握「通勤」給人的整體印象。

⑲行李架
㉕博愛座
㉖懸掛式廣告
⑳手拉吊環
㉔扶手
㉑孕婦
㉒老人
㉓中年男子

⑮ express ⑯ rapid train ⑰ special limited express ⑱ women-only car ⑲ rack ⑳ strap ㉑ pregnant woman ㉒ elderly person ㉓ middle-aged guy ㉔ handrail ㉕ priority seat ㉖ hanging poster

1 我通過行人穿越道（天橋）。
I cross at the crosswalk (pedestrian overpass).

2 我等紅綠燈。
I wait for the light to change.

3 我闖紅燈。
I cross against the light.

4 我和鄰居打招呼。
I say hello to my neighbors.

5 我跑到車站後上氣不接下氣。
I feel out of breath after running to the station.

❶「地下道」叫 underpass。
❷「紅綠燈變綠（紅）」就說成 The signal turns green (red)。
❹ 若是關係較親近的人，也可用 say hi to ~。
❺「上氣不接下氣；喘不過來」也可說成 be short of breath。

6 我上（下）車站樓梯。
I climb up (go down) the stairs in the station.

7 我用我的儲值票卡（悠遊卡）感應了一下驗票口。
I touch the ticket gate with my prepaid railway pass (EasyCard).

8 我被自動驗票口給攔下了。
I get stopped by the automatic ticket gate.

9 我替我的悠遊卡儲值。
I top up my EasyCard.

10 我選擇和平常不同的一條路線。
I take a different line than usual.

❻ 基本上室內的樓梯叫 stairs，戶外的樓梯叫 steps。
❼「驗票口」也叫做 ticket wicket。
❾ 儲值票卡也可稱為 top-up card。
❿ different than usual 是表示「與平日不同」之意。

11 我排隊等火車。
I stand in line and wait for the train.

12 我衝上火車。
I run onto the train.

13 我上（下）火車。
I get on (off) the train.

14 我被站務員推進車廂。
I get pushed in by a station employee.

15 我被擠到月台上，沒辦法再上車。
I get shoved out onto the platform and cannot get back on.

tips

⑪ 英式英語則說成 stand in a queue。

⑫ 「匆忙下車」可說成 rush out of the train。

⑭ 「被推進～」也可說成 get squeezed into~，而站務員也還有其它講法，如 station staff、station crew 等。

⑮ shove（注意其發音是：[ʃʌˋv]），為「用力推擠～」之意。

16 我把包包放在行李架上。
I put my bag on the rack.

17 我站在某個看來很快就要下車的人前面。
I stand in front of someone who looks likely to get off soon.

18 我抓住手拉吊環。
I hang onto the strap.

19 我在列車上打瞌睡。
I doze off on the train.

20 ＜列車緊急煞車時＞我失去平衡。
<When the train suddenly brakes> I lose my balance.

⓰「把包包忘在行李架上」說成 leave my bag on the rack，「把包包忘在列車上」則可用 forget my bag on the train 這樣的講法來表達。

⓳「打瞌睡」也可說成drop off、drift off。

⓴「保持平衡」說成 keep balance。

21 我撞到別人。
I bump into someone.

22 我踩到別人的腳。
I step on someone's foot.

23 我在擠得滿滿的列車上幾乎要窒息（骨折）了。
I nearly get suffocated (break a bone) on a packed train.

24 我讓座給一個老人（孕婦）。
I give up my seat to an elderly person (a pregnant woman).

25 我換車。
I change trains.

tips

㉑ bump into ~ 也可指「無意中遇到~」與 run into ~的意思相同。

㉒ 若是故意用力踩，則說成 stomp on ~。

㉓「擁擠的列車」說成 crowded train。另外也有更簡單的說法，如 busy train。

26 我走到女性專用車廂的乘車位置。
I move to the spot where a women-only car stops.

27 我通過驗票口。
I go through the ticket gate.

㉔ 用 elderly 這個字，會比 old 或 aged（老了的）更有禮貌。
㉕ 由於「換車；轉乘」一定與 2 台以上的列車有關，所以不說 change a train，而要用複數change trains。另外「轉乘～線」則說成 <u>change</u> / <u>transfer</u> to ~ line。
㉖「乘車位置」可說成 boarding point。

1　這個（鐵路）平交道很少打開。
This railroad crossing rarely opens.

2　平交道的警鈴已響起！我過得去嗎？！
The crossing bell is ringing already! Can I make it?!

3　還是在普通車上找個位子坐比較好，因為平快車真的很擠。
It's better to find a seat on a local train because that express is really crowded.

4　糟糕！我的包包被門夾住了。
Oh no! My bag's gotten stuck in the door[s]!

5　我運氣真好！找到了一個位子！
Lucky me! I found a seat!

6　這條路線延伸後，變得更加方便。
This line became more convenient after its expansion.

railroad crossing =（鐵路）平交道 cf. pedestrian crossing = 行人穿越道

rarely 是表示「不太～；很少～」等帶有否定意義的副詞。而 seldom 也代表類似意義，但是感覺較嚴肅。

---

crossing bell = 平交道警鈴 cf. crossing bar = 平交道柵欄

make it 是指「來得及」之意，在此就是指 Can I cross the railroad crossing before the [crossing] bar comes down?（我能在〔平交道〕柵欄放下前穿越平交道嗎？）的意思。

---

local train = 各站皆停的普通車／express [train] = 平快車 cf. limited express [train] = 特快車

此例句的前半部也可說成 I'm better off finding a seat ...。而 I had better find a seat ... 則指「我最好找到位子」，意思不一樣，故不用於此處。

---

have gotten stuck in ～ = 被～卡（夾）住

「被門夾住」也可說成 be caught in the door[s]。另外「我把包包拉進來」則說成 I pull my bag inside.。

Lucky me! / Lucky for me. / I'm in luck. = 我很幸運

這句也可說成 I didn't expect I'd find a seat.（我沒想到能找到位子）。此外，問人「我可以坐這兒嗎？」可以說 Do you mind if I sit here?。

---

convenient = 方便的／expansion = 延伸；擴張〔工程等〕

convenient 是以物體或情況為主詞的形容詞，故不能使用 ✕ I feel convenient with it.（我覺得它很方便）這種講法。

7 這條線常因機械故障而誤點。
This line is often delayed due to mechanical trouble.

8 不會吧，列車又減速了。
The train is reducing its speed. Not again.

9 今天列車停得很頻繁。
The train has been coming to a stop quite often today.

10 學校放假（暑假）期間，列車並不擁擠。
Trains are not busy during school holidays (the summer vacation).

11 這時候（在交通尖峰時間），我真希望自己是坐在往市外方向的列車上。
I wish I were on the outbound line at this time (during the rush hour).

12 我的耳機線脫落了。
My earphones came unplugged.

line =〔火車的〕路線 e.g. Western Line = 西部幹線／be delayed = 誤點／due to ~ = 由於~

其他可能的誤點原因還有：signal failure（信號故障）、accident causing injury or death（造成受傷或死亡的意外）等。

---

reduce [one's] speed = 減速／Not again. = 別再這樣了。

「減速」可說成 slow down，但不能說 × speed down。「嘿，又開始加速了」則是 Hey, it's speeding up again.。

---

come to a stop = 停止；停住／quite often = 很頻繁地

「列車因停止信號而突然停住」可說成 The train came to <u>a sudden</u> / <u>an abrupt</u> stop due to the stop signal.。

---

school holidays = 學校放的假 cf. summer <u>vacation</u>/<u>holidays</u>/<u>break</u> = 暑假（這幾個字感覺上長度不同：vacation > holidays > break）

busy 這個形容詞除了有「〔人〕很忙碌」的意思外，也常用來表示「〔商店・交通工具等〕很擁擠」之意，例如 Restaurants are busy because of Mother's Day.（餐廳因母親節而擠滿了人）。

---

the outbound line = 往市外（郊區）方向的路線 cf. the inbound line = 往市中心（鬧區）方向的路線

I wish I were ~（真希望我是～）這種句型，是藉著敘述與實際相反之狀況，來表達心中的願望。「早上（傍晚）的上下班交通尖峰期」就說成 morning (evening) rush hour。

---

earphones = 耳機（通常用複數）／unplugged = 被拔除的狀態；沒插上

come + 形容詞可表達「變成～的狀態」，例如 My shoelaces came loose on the packed train.（在擁擠的電車上我的鞋帶鬆了）。

13 那個人怎麼有辦法用那種姿勢看報紙？

How can that guy be reading a paper in that position?

14 看看那位老兄站著睡睡得多穩！

Look at how well that guy dozes while standing!

15 我的腳根本沒地方可站，都快跌倒了。

I'm falling over; there's no room for my feet.

16 他們如果能夠稍微移動一下，就可以再挪出一個位子。

They can make room for one more if they shift over a little.

17 那位小姐真有膽量，竟然敢在列車上畫全妝。

That lady's got a lot of nerve putting on full makeup on the train.

18 我得關手機。這裡是博愛座。

I've got to turn my cell off. This is a priority seat.

a paper = 一份報紙（可數名詞）cf. a lot of paper = 很多紙（不可數名詞）／in such a position = 以那種姿勢／position = 姿勢；狀態

How can S + V? 表示「S 怎麼有辦法做 V？」之意，而若用 How could ~? 便更提高了不可能的程度。

---

doze = 打瞌睡／while -ing = 一邊做～

Look at how S + V ~ 是「看看 S 是如何做 V 的」之意，例如 Look at how fast that elderly lady found a seat!（看看那老太太找到位子的速度可真快！）

---

fall over = 摔倒；跌倒／room = 空間、地方（不可數名詞）cf. a room/rooms = 房間

現在進行式（be -ing）除了可表達「現在正在做～」的意思外，也可表示「快要～」之意。這裡的 I'm falling over 就不是指「正在跌倒」，而是「快要跌倒」的意思。

---

make room for ~ = 為～騰出空間／shift over (= budge/scoot over) = 挪動

在車廂內想表達「可以請你往旁邊挪一下嗎？」的意思時，一般會說 Could you scoot over?。

---

have/have got a lot of nerve = 很有膽量／put on full makeup = 畫全妝；畫完整的妝／put on = 塗上〔化妝品〕

nerve 有「厚顏無恥；膽量」的意思，而利用 nerve 的常見句型還包括 have the nerve to ~（有做～的膽量）、You've got some nerve!（你好大的膽子！）等等。

---

have got to (= have to/need to) ~ = 必須～／turn ~ off = 關掉～的電源／cell (= cellphone) = 手機／priority seat = 博愛座

博愛座應優先禮讓給 elderly passengers（老年乘客）、handicapped passengers（殘障乘客）、expecting mothers（孕婦）、passengers accompanying small children（帶著幼童的乘客）等。

19 別把那個大包包放在地上！
Don't leave that big bag on the floor!

20 地下鐵實在是很吵。也許我該調大音量。
Maybe I better turn up the volume. The subway is so noisy.

21 我旁邊這傢伙的耳機漏出噪音來了！
Noise is leaking from the earphones of the guy beside me.

22 ＜搖搖晃晃站不穩時＞我不小心把粉底沾在某個中年男子的西裝上了。
<Staggering> I accidentally put some foundation on the suit of <u>some</u>/<u>a</u> middle-aged guy.

23 他一定是色狼……。
He's got to be a groper ...

24 真噁心。有把溼答答的傘黏在我手臂上。
That's gross. A wet umbrella's stuck against my arm.

leave ~ = 把～放著不管

「他的包包佔了太大空間」可說成 His bag takes up too much space.，而「那包包妨礙到大家」則說成 The bag is in everyone's way.。

Maybe I better ~ = 說不定我應該～/turn up the volume = 調大音量

I better ~ 為 I had better ~的簡略。而「轟隆隆的地鐵噪音讓我幾乎聽不見音樂」則可說成 I can hardly hear my music because of the rumbling subway noise.。

---

leak from ~ = 從～漏出來/beside ~ = 在～旁邊

這種情況也可說成 The guy next to me is listening to music too loudly. I can hear what he's listening to.（我旁邊的人聽音樂開得太大聲。我都聽得到他在聽什麼）。

---

accidentally = 意外地；不小心地/foundation =〔化妝品的〕粉底/middle-aged = 中年的

「故意地」，則用 on purpose 來表達，例如 This man is leaning against me. He must be doing it on purpose.（這個男人一直往我這邊靠過來。他一定是故意的）。

---

have got to ~ = 一定是～/groper = 伸鹹豬手的色狼 cf.「變態」叫 pervert；「性騷擾者」或「猥褻者」叫 molester

have got to ~（一定是～；應該是～）這種講法很常出現在比較輕鬆的對話中，其意義與 must（一定是）類似，例如 I've got to be on the wrong train.（我一定是坐錯車了）。

---

gross = 噁心的/~ stick against ... = ～黏在……上

gross表示「令人噁心」之意。另外，clammy 也可表達「〔黏黏的〕好噁心」之意，例如 The handrail is sticky and clammy.（扶手黏答答的好噁心）。

25 喂，別把報紙攤得那麼大。
Hey, don't open your paper so wide here.

26 我旁邊的小姐靠在我身上。我的肩膀好痛。
The lady next to me is leaning against me. My shoulder hurts.

27 我隔壁的傢伙嘴好臭。
The guy next to me has terrible breath.

28 哇，那傢伙真酷！
Wow, isn't that guy cool!

29 現在所有車站和列車都禁煙了。
Every station and every train is non-smoking these days.

30 冷氣太強了。我可能會感冒！
The air conditioner is way too strong. I might catch a cold!

open ~ wide = 把～攤開拉大

hey（喂）在此是喚起對方注意用的感嘆詞。另外，也經常用在非正式的問候句中，例如 hey, what's up?（嘿，最近如何？）。

---

next to ~ = ～旁邊的／lean against ~ = 靠著～／hurt = 使疼痛；感覺疼痛

「往後靠」說成 lean back，例如 I lean back and bang my head against the window.（我往後靠，頭撞到了窗戶）。

---

terrible = 很糟的；很嚇人的

要陳述「（人）的～是很……的」這類句子時，通常會用 have ~ 來表達，例如 That guy has a strange hair style.（那傢伙的髮型很怪）。

---

cool =〔人〕酷 cf. ugly = 醜

此例句用了 not，乍看之下像是否定疑問句，但其實是一種強調肯定意義（That guy is cool.）的表達方式。

---

non-smoking = 禁煙的／these days = 近來；現在

「你可以不要在這裡抽煙嗎？這裡是禁煙車廂」就說成 Would you mind not smoking here? It's a non-smoking car.。

---

way = 遠遠地（副詞）／air conditioner = 空調；冷氣／catch a cold = 感冒

「可以請你調弱（關掉）冷氣嗎？」就說成 Could you turn down (turn off) the air conditioner?

31 ＜在擠滿了人的列車上＞下一站不知道下不下得了車？
<On a jam-packed train> Will I be able to get out at the next station?

32 呼！我差一點就坐過站了。
Whew! I almost missed my stop.

33 走在我前面的是我們經理。我該跟他打個招呼。
That's my manager walking ahead of me. I should say hello to him.

34 末班車可能已經開走了！
The last train might have left already!

35 糟糕！我錯過了末班車。
Shoot! I've missed the last train.

36 末班車裡有一大堆醉鬼。
There are loads of drunks on the last train.

be able to ～ = 能夠～／get out = 出去；逃出

「下車」通常用 get off（e.g. I get off the train.），但從擠滿了人的車廂下車時，會有一種「逃出來」的感覺，因此用 get out 更能傳達該氣氛。

---

whew = 呼（表示疲勞的感嘆詞）／almost = 差一點就～／miss = 錯過～

將副詞 almost 改為 nearly（幾乎），說成 I nearly missed my stop.，意思幾乎一模一樣。

---

manager = 經理／ahead of ～ = 在～前方／say hello to ～ = 跟～打招呼

manager除了指「經理」外，也常用來指藝人或運動員的「經紀人」。

---

the last train = 末班車 cf. the first train = 首班車

might have + 過去分詞，表示「可能已經～了」的意思，例如 The first train might have arrived already.（首班車可能已經到了）。

Shoot! = 糟糕！

shoot 是用來表達吃驚或焦慮惱怒的感嘆詞，用以代替粗俗的 shit（狗屎）這個字。

---

loads of ～ = 一大堆的～／drunk = 喝醉的人（名詞）

loads of ～ 的意思和 lots of ～ (= a lot of ～) 相同，但更為口語化。就有點像中文裡「一大堆的」和「許多的」之差異。

Skit  通勤篇 ──────────

早上的通勤電車真讓人受夠了

Man: **Good morning. How are you today?**

Woman: **Terrible❶! I hate taking❷ the train in the morning.**

M: **What happened?**

W: **First of all❸, my bag got stuck in the door, then someone's wet umbrella was stuck against my arm.**

M: **Oh, I hate it when that happens.**

W: **I was hanging onto the strap but I lost my balance when the train suddenly braked, and I bumped into someone and stepped on his foot. He gave me a really nasty look❹, but it wasn't my fault❺!**

M: **Of course not.**

W: **And the air conditioner was way too strong. I think I caught a cold.**

M: **That's not good.**

W: **And noise was leaking from the earphones of the guy beside me. And the guy standing on the other side had terrible breath. I think he must have had❻ garlic for breakfast!**

M: **That's really annoying❼. They should make garlic illegal❽.**

W: **Ha-ha. The worst part was I almost missed my stop, and now I'm in a terrible mood❾.**

M: **Here. Have a doughnut. That'll make you feel better❿.**

W: **Now you're trying to make me fat. What an awful day!**

男子：早安！今天如何？

女子：糟透了！我最討厭搭早上的電車了。

男：發生了什麼事？

女：首先，我的包包被門夾住 。 然後有個人溼答答的雨傘又黏著我的手臂。

男：噢，那真的很討厭。

女：我抓著手拉吊環，但是當列車緊急煞車的時候，我失去平衡，撞到別人，還踩到他的腳。他狠狠地瞪了我一眼，可是那又不是我的錯！

男：當然不是妳的錯。

女：然後冷氣又太強。我想我感冒了。

男：真糟。

女：另外我隔壁那傢伙的耳機漏出噪音，而站在另一旁的傢伙又有口臭。我想他早餐一定吃了大蒜！

男：那真的是很討人厭。應該要立法禁止大蒜才對。

女：哈哈。最糟的是，我差一點就坐過站，所以現在心情超差的。

男：來，吃個甜甜圈。這能讓妳心情變好。

女：現在你又想讓我變胖。今天真的是糟糕透頂了！

【單字片語】

❶ terrible：糟透了
❷ hate -ing：討厭做～
❸ first of all：首先
❹ give ~ a nasty look：狠狠地瞪～一眼
❺ be one's fault：～的過錯

❻ he must have had ~：他一定吃了～
❼ annoying：惱人的；討厭的
❽ illegal：違法的；非法的
❾ in a terrible mood：心情非常不好
❿ feel better：心情變好；感覺好些

Quick Check

讓我們一起來複習本章所介紹過的句型！請依據以下中文句子的意思，來完成對應的英文句子。（答案就在本頁最下方。）

❶ 我闖紅燈。→P042

I ( ) ( ) the light.

❷ 我用我的儲值票卡感應了一下驗票口。→P043

I ( ) the ( ) ( ) with my ( ) ( )
( ).

❸ 我被擠到月台上，沒辦法再上車。→P044

I get ( ) ( ) onto the ( ) and cannot ( )
( ) ( ).

❹ 我走到女性專用車廂的乘車位置。→P047

I move to the ( ) ( ) a ( ) car ( ).

❺ 在普通車上找個位子坐比較好，因為平快車真的很擠。→P048

It's better to ( ) a ( ) on a ( ) train because that
( ) is really ( ).

❻ 這條線常因機械故障而誤點。→P050

This ( ) is often ( ) ( ) to ( ) ( ).

❼ 他們如果能稍微移動一下，就可再挪出一個位子。→P052

They can ( ) ( ) for ( ) ( ) if they
( ) ( ) a little.

❽ ＜搖搖晃晃站不穩時＞我不小心把粉底沾在某個中年男子的西裝上了。→P054

I ( ) ( ) some ( ) ( ) the suit of a
( ) ( ).

❾ 喂，別把報紙攤得那麼大。→P056

( ), don't ( ) your ( ) so ( ) here.

❿ 末班車可能已經開走了！→P058

The ( ) train ( ) ( ) ( ) already!

---

❶ cross/against ❷ touch/ticket/gate/
prepaid/railway/pass ❸ shoved/out/
platform/get/back/on ❹ spot/where/
women-only/stops ❺ find/seat/local/
express/crowded ❻ line/delayed/ due/

mechanical/trouble ❼ make/room/one/
more/shift/over ❽ accidentally/put/
foundation/on/middle-aged/guy ❾ Hey/
open/paper/wide ❿ last/might/have/left

chapter 3 Housework

家事

洗衣、打掃、煮飯、購物……
做家事用的工具及物品多不勝數，
家事的份量與種類也不容小覷。
近年來，做家事甚至融入環保概念呢！
本篇有許多英文句型，
都很適合邊做家事邊述說喔。

chapter ❸ Housework

Words 單字篇

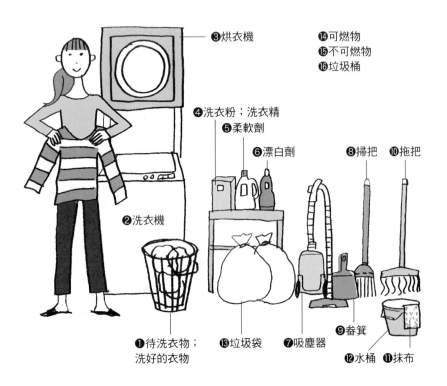

❸烘衣機
⓮可燃物
⓯不可燃物
⓰垃圾桶
❹洗衣粉；洗衣精
❺柔軟劑
❻漂白劑
❽掃把　❿拖把
❷洗衣機
❾畚箕
❶待洗衣物；
洗好的衣物
⓭垃圾袋　❼吸塵器
⓬水桶　⓫抹布

❶ laundry　❷ washing machine　❸ dryer　❹ laundry detergent
❺ softener　❻ bleach　❼ vacuum cleaner　❽ broom　❾ dustpan
❿ mop　⓫ rag　⓬ bucket　⓭ garbage bag　⓮ combustible

首先，讓我們透過各種物品的名稱，來掌握「家事」給人的整體印象。

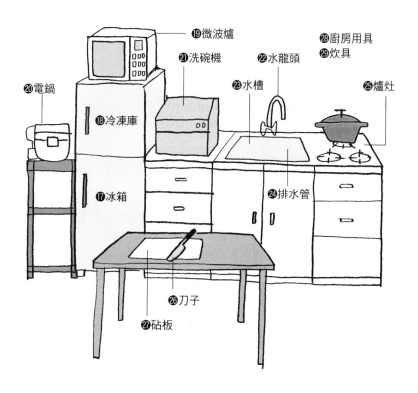

⑲微波爐
㉘廚房用具
㉙炊具
㉑洗碗機
㉒水龍頭
㉓水槽
㉕爐灶
⑳電鍋
⑱冷凍庫
⑰冰箱
㉔排水管
㉖刀子
㉗砧板

⑮ non-combustible ⑯ garbage can ⑰ refrigerator ⑱ freezer
⑲ microwave ⑳ ricecooker ㉑ dishwasher ㉒ faucet ㉓ sink ㉔ drain
㉕ stove ㉖ knife ㉗ cutting board ㉘ kitchen utensils ㉙ cookware

1 我把待洗衣物放進洗衣機裡。
I put my laundry in the washing machine.

2 我利用洗澡水來洗衣服。
**I do the laundry <u>with/</u>
<u>using</u> the bath water.**

3 洗襯衫之前，我會先把襯衫泡在水裡。
I soak the shirt in water before washing.

4 我晾乾衣服。
**I hang the laundry up
to dry.**

5 我陰乾衣服。
**I let the <u>laundry/clothes</u>
dry in the shade.**

tips

❶ laundry 是「待洗衣物；洗好的衣物」之總稱。「將洗好的衣物從洗衣機拿出來」就說成 take the laundry out of the washing machine。

❷ 「〔洗衣用的〕清潔劑」，亦即洗衣粉、洗衣精等，叫做 [laundry] detergent，而「柔軟劑」是 softener。

❸ soak 是指「浸泡」。而「漂白襯衫」則說成 clean the shirt with bleach。

6 我把洗好的衣物放進烘乾機裡。
I put the laundry in the dryer.

7 我折衣服。
I fold the clothes.

8 我燙衣服。
I iron the clothes.

9 我整理衣物以換季。
I rearrange my wardrobe for the new season.

10 我把冬天的衣服送去乾洗。
I take my winter clothes to the dry cleaner's.

❹「晾墊被」可說成 air out the futons,「把洗好的衣服拿進來」則是
take in the laundry。
❺「在太陽下曬衣服」可說成 dry the clothes in the sun。
❻「烘乾機」也可拼成 drier。「用烘乾機烘乾」則說成 tumble-dry。
❾ wardrobe 指「個人所擁有全部服裝」(總稱)。
❿ 乾洗店也可說成 the cleaner's 或 dry-cleaning shop。

11 我出門採購食物。
I go shopping for food.

12 我尋找有打折的（特價）商品。
I look for items at discount prices (bargain prices).

13 我牢記商品的最低價格。
I keep the item's lowest price in mind.

14 我在超市的收銀台前排隊結帳。
I wait in the checkout line at the supermarket.

15 我確認找的錢數目正確。
I make sure I got the right change.

tips

❶ 「列出購物清單」說成 <u>make</u> / <u>write</u> a shopping list。
❷ look for ~ 就是「尋找～」之意，而 items 則指「物品；商品」。
❸ keep ~ in mind 是「牢記～」之意。
❹ line 是指「排隊的隊伍」。「收銀台」說成 <u>checkout counter</u> / <u>cash register</u>，「收銀員」則說成 cashier。另外 express

16 我整理冰箱裡的東西。
I sort out the contents of the refrigerator.

17 我用剩餘食材做晚餐。
I make dinner with what's left.

18 我試做在電視上看到的（在網站上找到的）新食譜。
I try a new recipe I saw on TV (found on a website).

19 我磨利菜刀。
I sharpen a knife.

20 我清理餐桌。
I clear the table.

counter 則是指購買的商品數量在特定數量以下者專用的結帳櫃檯。
⓰ sort out 是「整理；清理」之意。另外，「冰箱」也可說成 fridge。
⓱ make dinner 也可說成 fix dinner，而 what's left 就是「剩下的東西」。
⓴ clear 是指將表面的東西收走，亦即「清理」之意，而 clean 則是將髒污擦除，亦即「弄乾淨」之意。另外，「擦桌子」是 wipe the table。

21 我收拾房間。
I tidy up the room.

22 我除去家具上的灰塵。
I dust the furniture.

23 我讓房間通風。
I air out the room.

24 我用吸塵器吸地板（清房間）。
I vacuum the floor (room).

25 我用濕抹布擦地板。
I wipe the floor with a wet rag.

tips

❷❶ tidy up 是「收拾；整理」之意。若要表達去除髒污，並「弄乾淨、清掃」之意時，請用 clean。

❷❸ air out (= let some fresh air into the room) 是「通風換氣」之意。

❷❹「吸塵器」叫 vacuum cleaner；「雞毛撢子」是 duster；「掃把」是 broom，而「拖把」則為 mop。

26 我用拖把拖地。
I mop the floor.

27 我替地板打蠟。
I wax the floor.

28 我清除浴室裡的黴菌。
I clean off the mold in the bathroom.

29 我重新裝飾我的房間（房子）。
I redecorate my room (house).

30 我進行歲末大掃除。
I clean the house at the end of the year.

㉕「洗抹布」可說成 rinse [out] the rag，「擰乾抹布」則是 wring [out] the rag。

㉗「替地板打蠟」也可說成 polish the floor with wax。

㉙「重新裝飾」也可用 redo 或 rearrange。

㉚ 美國是在 4 月進行大掃除，故說成 spring cleaning。

31 我用小蘇打和醋進行環保式的清潔。
I do eco-friendly cleaning with baking soda and vinegar.

32 我洗碗前會先將碗盤徹底刮乾淨。
I scrape the dishes thoroughly before I wash them.

33 我把一疊舊報紙拿出去回收。
I take a stack of old newspapers out for recycling.

34 我查閱塑膠類垃圾的回收日。
I check the garbage collection day for plastics.

35 我打掃院子。
I sweep the yard.

tips

㉛ 「eco」是 ecology（生態學）的縮寫。英語通常用 eco-friendly 來表達「環保的」之意，而「環保商品」則說成 green <u>goods</u>/<u>products</u>。

㉜ scrape 是「把～刮（擦）乾淨」之意。另外，「洗碗機」叫 dishwasher。

㉝ a stack of ~ 是「疊成一堆的～」。

36 我替庭院除草。
I weed my garden.

37 我在庭院裡種植香草類植物。
I grow herbs in my garden.

38 我裝配電線。
I wire the cables/connect the wires.

39 我付帳單。
I pay my bills.

40 我記錄家庭開支。
I keep records of household expenses.

❸❹ 「垃圾」可說成 trash 或 rubbish。「把垃圾拿出去；去倒垃圾」說成 take out the garbage，而「將可燃和不可燃垃圾分類」則是 separate the garbage into combustible and noncombustible。

❸❺ sweep 是「〔用掃把或刷子等〕清掃」之意。

❸❻ 「拔除雜草」可說成 pull up the weeds，而「修剪草坪」則叫 mow the lawn。

❸❾ bill 就是「帳單」，而「收帳員」則叫 <u>bill/money</u> collector。

1　待洗衣物堆積如山。
The laundry is piling up.

2　今天很適合洗衣服。
It's a good day to do the laundry.

3　別把襪子脫成裡頭朝外就不管了。
Don't leave your socks inside out.

4　糟糕！我的白襯衫被染成粉紅色了。
Oh, no! My white shirt is stained pink.

5　我要把和服拿出來吹吹風。
I'm going to air out the kimono.

6　天啊！我的外套被蛀蟲咬出洞來了！
My goodness! My coat has got moth holes!

laundry = 待洗衣物 e.g. a load of laundry = 一批待洗衣物／pile up = 堆積如山；越積越多 e.g. pile up high = 堆得高高的

這句也可說成 I have a lot of washing to do.（我有很多衣物待洗）。

It's a good day to ~ (= It's a great day to ~) = 今天很適合～／do the laundry (= do the washing) = 洗衣服

「晾乾衣物」說成 dry laundry，「在外面晾乾」則說成 hang the laundry out to dry，而「在室內晾乾」則是 hang the laundry inside。

---

leave = 放著～的狀態不管／inside out = 裡頭朝外的 cf. upside down = 上下顛倒的

襪子都是成對的，所以 a sock 是指一隻襪子，而「一雙襪子」應說成 a pair of socks。

---

shirt = 襯衫／stain = 被～沾汙；被～染色

要表達「染上～色」就用 be stained +～色。而「有色衣物請分開洗滌」這樣的衣物處理指示則說成 Wash colors separately.。

---

air out = 讓～通風；讓～透氣

kimono 已成為正式的英語單字，但若對方聽不懂，只要用 traditional Japanese-style clothing / garment 來解釋即可。而一般衣服就用 clothes。

My goodness! = 天啊！／moth hole = 蟲咬的洞 e.g. get moth holes = 被蛀蟲咬出洞來

這句也可說成 Moths ate my coat!（我的外套被蟲咬了！）。另外「防蟲蛀的」（形容詞）則叫 mothproof。

7 我今天不想做晚飯。
I don't feel up to making dinner today.

8 或許我可以叫點什麼食物外送。
Maybe I'll order out for something to eat.

9 今天的餐點一點都不麻煩！
Today's meal is fuss-free!

10 我實在想不出今天要吃什麼。有了！讓我上網查查！
I can't come up with any ideas for what to eat today. I know! Let me search the Internet!

11 現在秋刀魚正當季。
Saury is in season now.

12 這超過保存期限了，不知道還可以〔吃〕嗎？
This has passed the best-before date, but is it OK [to eat]?

don't feel up to ~ = 不想～；沒有做～的心情

feel up to ~ 通常用於否定句；若想表達「覺得想做～」之意，就用 I feel like ～。另外「做晚餐真的很麻煩」則可説成 It's such a chore making dinner.。

---

order out for ~ = 叫～的外送 cf. [home-]delivery service = 外送；宅配服務／something to eat = 一些吃的東西

這句也可説成 I will get food delivered.（我可以叫食物外送）。deliver 是「配送」之意，而 Do you deliver? 就是「你們可以外送嗎？」。

---

fuss = 忙亂；緊張不安／~ -free = 沒有～ cf. calorie-free = 零熱量的／sugar-free = 無糖

fuss-free 是指「輕鬆愉快的；不麻煩的」。而「省事」可説成 save [one's] trouble，至於相反的「費工」則可説成 with [an] effort。

---

come up with = 想出（點子）／what to eat = 要吃什麼／I know! = 有了！／search the Internet/Net = 上網搜尋

「想不出來要煮什麼」就説成 I can't think of what to cook.。

---

in season = 當季的；正值盛產季節 e.g. vegetables (fruit) in season = 當季的蔬菜（水果）

「現在是秋刀魚最好吃的季節」可説成 It's the season for delicious saury fish.。秋刀魚也可説成 skipper，日文則叫Sanma。

---

pass = 超過～／the best-before date (= the used-by date) = 保存期限 cf. expiration date = 到期日

「你覺得還可以吃嗎？」説成 Do you think it's OK to eat?.。「過期食品」可説成 expired food。

13 噢，有顆番茄爛掉了。

Oh, I've found a rotten tomato.

14 我都避免油炸食物，因為事後清理很麻煩。

I avoid deep-frying because cleaning up afterwards is so much work.

15 我聞到了燒焦的味道！

I smell something burning!

16 自製的食物結果還是比現成的食品貴。

Homemade food turned out to be more costly than ready-made food.

17 我要先留點菜當明天的午餐。

I'll set aside some food for tomorrow's lunch.

18 如果我事先做些菜，對平日會很有幫助。

It will be very helpful on weekdays if I cook something ahead.

rotten = 爛掉的 cf. rot = （肉、蔬菜等）腐爛或腐敗／spoil = （食物）壞掉／go bad = 腐壞；壞掉

avoid = 避免〜／deep-fry = 用〔很多〕油來酥炸 cf. fry = 熱炒／stir-fry = 拌炒／afterwards = 事後

這句也可說成 I don't make fried food because cleaning up afterward is so hard.，而 fried food 就是「油炸的食物」。

smell something 〜 = 聞到一些〜的味道 e.g. Do you smell something? = 你有聞到些什麼味道嗎？／burn = 燃燒；燒焦

這句也可說成 Something is burning!（有東西燒焦了！）。

homemade = 自製的 e.g. homemade apple pie = 自製蘋果派／turn out to 〜 = 結果是〜／costly (= expensive) = 價格高的；貴的／ready-made food (= prepared food) = 現成食品

set aside 〜 = 把〜分出來

此句後半也可改為「為了裝明天的便當…」... to put in tomorrow's lunchbox。另外「做（裝）便當」則是 I make (pack) my lunch.。

helpful = 有幫助的；有利的／weekdays = 平日 cf. weekend = 週末／cook = 烹調〜；煮〜／ahead = 事先

「菜餚」是 dishes，而主菜就叫 main dish，配菜則是 side dishes。

19 我放了一晚的咖哩味道真是棒極了。
The curry that I left overnight tastes superb!

20 我會把剩飯冷凍起來。
I'll freeze the leftover rice.

21 呃！我在冰箱深處發現了一個 3 年前的食品罐頭。
Ugh! I found a three-year-old can of food deep inside the fridge.

22 從角落的水槽濾網處傳來一陣噁心的臭味。
A nasty odor is coming from the sink strainer in the corner.

23 我的手因為使用洗潔劑而變粗糙了！
My hands got rough from using detergent!

24 這個洗潔劑無法去除排水管裡黏黏滑滑的東西。
This detergent can't get rid of the slime in the drain.

overnight ＝ 過夜／taste ＝ 吃起來；嚐起來／superb ＝ 棒極了

「讓～靜置一夜」可說成 let ~ stand overnight。而「咖哩飯」不要說成 curry rice，正統英語應說成 curry and rice 或 curried rice。

---

freeze ＝ 把～冷凍起來 cf. freezer ＝ 冷凍庫／refrigerator ＝ 冰箱／refrigerate ＝ 將～冷藏／leftover ＝ 吃剩的；剩餘的

這句也可說成 I'll put the rest of the meal in the freezer.（我會把剩飯放進冷凍庫）。

---

can of food ＝ 食品罐頭 cf. canned ＝ 裝成罐頭的／deep inside ~ ＝ 在～的內部深處／fridge (= refrigerator) ＝ 冰箱

three-year-old 就是指「經過了 3 年的」，是一個形容詞。

---

nasty ＝ 噁心的；討厭的／odor ＝ 臭味；臭氣 cf. foul odor ＝ 惡臭／sink ＝ 廚房水槽／strainer ＝ 濾網；過濾器

smell「氣味」可用於好的氣味，也可用於不好的氣味，但 odor 主要只用於不好的氣味。

---

hand ＝ 手 cf. palm ＝ 手掌／finger ＝ 手指／nail ＝ 指甲／rough ＝ 粗糙的；不平的 e.g. rough and dry ＝ 又粗又乾／detergent ＝ 洗潔劑 cf. soap ＝ 肥皂

「柔細的手」可說成 soft and smooth hand，而「保護手部以免～」則說成 protect hands from ~。

---

get rid of ~ ＝ 去除～／slime ＝ 黏黏滑滑的東西／drain ＝ 排水管；排水設備

「排水管塞住了」說成 The drain is clogged.，而「清潔排水管」則是 clean the drain。

25 如果我在這時候使用吸塵器，可能會造成不少困擾。
It would cause a lot of trouble if I vacuum at this hour.

26 無論我清掃得多勤，我家狗兒的毛依舊到處都是。
My dog's hair is all over the place no matter how often I clean it up.

27 糟糕！我婆婆檢查了櫃子，看上面有沒有灰塵。
Oh, no! My mother-in-law checked for dust on the shelf.

28 我真不敢相信短短一週內就能累積這麼多灰塵。
I can't believe how much dust we get in just a week.

29 灰塵在木質地板上看來更是明顯。
Dust is more visible on the wooden floor.

30 依據風水，我一定要保持浴廁清潔才行。
According to feng shui, I should definitely keep the bathroom clean.

cause trouble＝造成困擾／vacuum＝使用吸塵器

此句也可改用 It would be disturbing if～（如果～的話，會打擾別人）的句型。如果 at this hour 是指清晨（深夜）的話，便可說成 at this hour of the morning (night)。

---

hair＝毛（集合詞） cf. a hair＝1 根毛／all over the place＝散佈各處 e.g. leave things all over the place＝東西四處亂丟／no matter how often ～＝無論多麼常做～

---

mother-in-law＝婆婆；岳母／dust＝灰塵 cf. dusty＝滿是灰塵的

～-in-law 是用來表示法律上的（因結婚而形成的）親戚關係。「兒子的妻子」叫 daughter-in-law，「公公；岳父」叫 father-in-law，而所有姻親則統稱為 in-laws。

I can't believe ～＝我真不敢相信～／in just a week＝僅僅一星期內

這句也可說成 I can't believe how much dust has gathered in just a week.

---

visible＝眼睛可見的／wooden floor (＝ wood floor)＝木質地板

而「地毯」叫 carpet，「鋪有地毯的房間」則叫 carpeted room。「榻榻米」可說成 *tatami* / *straw-mat floor*。

---

according to ～＝依據～／feng shui＝風水（一種中國傳統的運勢占卜）／definitely＝一定；必定

「基於風水」是 based on feng shui，而「祈求好運」說成 pray for better fortune/luck，至於「吉祥；吉利」則說成 good luck/lucky。

31 油漬很難清除。
Grease stains are tough to remove.

32 我看到磁磚接縫處有黑色髒污。
I see dark smudges between the tiles.

33 我們的收納空間不夠。
We don't have enough storage space.

34 螢光燈在閃，是該替換的時候了。
The fluorescent light is flickering. It's time to replace it.

35 我們的衛生紙快用完了。
We are running out of toilet paper.

36 現在正在進行限時提供的裝到滿特賣活動。
There's a limited offer on an all-you-can-carry sale.

grease stain = 油漬 cf. greasy dirt = 油垢／greasy = 油膩的／tough to ~ = 很難~／remove = 去除

本句也可說成 Grease stains are hard to get rid of.。

---

smudge (= dirty spot) = 髒污；汙點

這句也可說成 I see dirty spots around the tiles.。「接縫」直譯成英語就是 joint，不過用 <u>between</u> / <u>around</u> the tiles 來指稱「磁磚之間／周圍」的髒汙，會更容易理解。

---

enough = 足夠的／storage = 儲藏；收納〔庫〕cf. store = 存放~／space = 空間

「你都把衣服收在哪兒？」就說成 Where do you store your clothes?

---

fluorescent light = 螢光燈 cf. [electrical] light bulb = 〔電〕燈泡／incandescent <u>light</u>/<u>lamp</u> = 白熾燈／flicker = 閃爍／it's time to ~ = 該是~的時候了

「燈泡燒掉了」說成 The light bulb has burnt out.，而「燈泡不亮了」則說成 The light is not working.。

---

run out of ~ = 用完~；耗盡~

在此以現在進行式 be -ing 表達「現在快要成為那種狀態了」之意。而「我們的衛生紙已經用完了」則可說成 We don't have any more toilet paper.。「一卷備用衛生紙」叫 a spare roll of toilet paper。

---

limited offer = 限時優惠；限量優惠／all-you-can-carry = 只要帶得走就全部讓你帶回家的 cf. all-you-can-eat = 吃到飽／all-you-can-drink = 無限暢飲

就英語表達而言，all-you-can-carry 會比 all-you-can-pack 更為自然。

37 我集到〔折價卡的〕點數了！
I've earned points [on my discount card] !

38 今天可獲得比平常多 5 倍的點數，所以我要去多買一些。
Today I can earn five times more points than usual, so I'm going to buy a lot!

39 冷凍食品打 6 折。
Frozen food is 40 percent off.

40 我們家的家庭開支記錄很不精準。
Our household expense records are very sloppy.

41 我們這個月必須盡量減少開銷。
We must cut back on spending as much as possible this month.

42 垃圾分類這麼麻煩。我很懷疑垃圾是否真的有被回收再利用。
Separating garbage is so complicated. I wonder if it's really recycled.

earn points = 集點；累積點數／discount card (= reward card) = 折價卡；優惠卡

「累積到的點數」說成 accumulated points，而「優待券；折價券」叫 coupon，「商品兌換券」則叫 voucher。

~ times = ～倍的／buy a lot = 買很多

~ times more than usual 表達「比平常多～倍」之意。而「點數變 2 倍（3 倍）」則說成 The points will be doubled (tripled).。

---

frozen food = 冷凍食品／~ percent off = 折價百分之～ cf. half off = 半價的

請注意，英文的 ~ percent off 是指減價的百分比，而中文的「～折」則是指減價後剩餘價格的百分比，兩者剛好相反。「折價〔百分之～〕販賣（購買）」說成 sell (buy) at a [~ percent] discount。另外，「將冷凍食品解凍」可說成 thaw frozen food。

---

household expense records = 家庭開支記錄 cf. household account = 家計／sloppy = 隨便的；草率的

very sloppy 也可改為 far from precise（很不精準）。

---

cut back on ~ = 減少～；削減～／spending = 開支；消費

這句也可說成 We must cut down on household expenses.。另外，「省吃儉用」可以說成 tighten our belts（勒緊褲腰帶）。

---

separate = 將～分類／garbage = 垃圾（集合詞）／complicated = 複雜的／I wonder if ~ = 我懷疑是否～／recycle = 回收再利用 e.g. recycled paper = 再生紙

「垃圾」也叫做 trash 或 rubbish。

43 我聽說這種洗潔劑不環保。
I hear this detergent is not environmentally-friendly.

44 家事是永遠都做不完的。
Household chores go on forever.

45 真希望我們雇得起管家。
I wish we could afford [to hire] a housekeeper.

46 我們平均分攤家務。
We divide household chores equally.

I hear ～ = 我聽說～／environmentally-friendly = 環保的 cf. earth-friendly = 對地球有助益的

「對環境有不良影響」可説成 have an adverse impact on the environment。

---

household chores (= housework) = 家事 cf. chores = 日常雜務／go on forever = 永無止盡

這句也可説成 Housework is never done. 或 Housework never ends.。

---

afford =〔財力上〕能負擔～／hire = 雇用／housekeeper (= domestic help) = 管家；幫傭

I wish ～ 的 wish 是用來表達不太可能實現的願望；I hope ～ 則用來表達可能實現的願望。

---

divide ～ equally = 平均分攤～

此句若是由先生説，應用 My wife and I ～，若是由妻子説，則用 My husband and I ～ 這類更明確的説法。請特別注意在英語中，通常不説 I and ～，而會將 I 置於後方，説成 ～ and I。

Skit  家事篇

笨手笨腳的老公能做什麼家事呢?

Woman 1: **Hi, Marie. How was your weekend?**

Woman 2: **I was really busy. I had to rearrange my wardrobe for the new season.**

W1: **Yes, you look kind of❶ tired❷.**

W2: **I am. I had to air out the clothes first. Plus, the laundry was piling up. And the dog's hair gets all over the place no matter how often I clean it up.**

W1: **Doesn't your husband help you? My husband and I divide household chores equally.**

W2: **Oh, he tries to help but he's useless. When he clears the table, he breaks the dishes. When he irons the clothes, he burns them. I wish we could afford to hire a housekeeper.**

W1: **I know how you feel. We have to cut back on spending this month. I do the laundry using bath water and look for items at discount prices.**
Oh, did you see today's newspaper? Frozen food is 40 percent off at Buy A Lot supermarket.

W2: **But you have to wait in the checkout line forever at Buy A Lot.**

W1: **Why don't you❸ make your husband do it?**

W2: **Good idea! He couldn't possibly❹ mess that up❺!**

女子 1：嗨，瑪莉。週末過得如何？

女子 2：我忙翻了。我得整理衣物以換季。

女 1：是啊，妳看起來真的有點兒累。

女 2：我是很累啊。首先我必須把衣服拿出來吹吹風。還有，待洗衣物也已經堆積如山。而且無論我清掃得多麼勤，依舊到處都是狗毛。

女 1：妳老公都不幫忙嗎？我老公和我都平均分攤家務。

女 2：噢，他有試著幫忙，但是他很沒用。他清理餐桌會打破盤子，燙衣服會燙到燒焦。真希望我們雇得起管家。

女 1：我懂妳的感受。我們這個月必須省吃儉用才行。我用洗澡水洗衣服，而買東西都找特價品。
噢，妳有看今天的報紙嗎？Buy A Lot 超市的冷凍食品打 6 折耶。

女 2：可是在 Buy A Lot 超市結帳都要等好久。

女 1：何不叫妳老公去？

女 2：好主意！這種事他總不可能搞砸吧！

【單字片語】

❶ kind of：有點兒；有些
❷ look tired：看起來很累
❸ Why don't you ~：你何不～？
❹ couldn't possibly ~：怎樣都不可能～
❺ mess ~ up：搞砸～；把～弄得一團糟

Quick Check

讓我們一起來複習本章所介紹過的句型！請依據以下中文句子的意思，來完成對應的英文句子。（答案就在本頁最下方。）

❶ 洗襯衫之前，我會先把襯衫泡在水裡。 →P066

I ( ) the shirt ( ) ( ) before ( ).

❷ 我整理冰箱裡的東西。 →P069

I ( ) ( ) the contents of the ( ).

❸ 我收拾房間。 →P070

I ( ) ( ) the room.

❹ 我把一疊舊報紙拿出去回收。 →P072

I take ( ) ( ) ( ) old newspapers ( ) for ( ).

❺ 別把襪子脫成裡頭朝外就不管了。 →P074

Don't ( ) your socks ( ) ( ).

❻ 我實在想不出今天要吃什麼。有了！讓我上網查查！ →P076

I can't ( ) ( ) ( ) any ( ) for what to eat today. I ( )! Let me ( ) ( ) ( )!

❼ 現在秋刀魚正當季。 →P076

Saury ( ) ( ) ( ) now.

❽ 噢，有顆番茄爛掉了。 →P078

Oh, I've ( ) a ( ) tomato.

❾ 依據風水，我一定要保持浴廁清潔才行。 →P082

( ) ( ) feng shui, I should ( ) ( ) the bathroom ( ).

❿ 我們的衛生紙快用完了。 →P084

We ( ) ( ) ( ) ( ) toilet paper.

---

❶ soak / in / water / washing ❷ sort / out / refrigerator ❸ tidy / up ❹ a / stack / of / out / recycling ❺ leave / inside / out ❻ come / up / with / ideas / know / search / the / Internet ❼ is / in / season ❽ found / rotten ❾ According / to / definitely / keep / clean ❿ are / running / out / of

chapter 4

Working at the Office

辦公室工作

出社會後,大部分人都會選擇去公司上班。
每天和電話及各式文件搏鬥,
還有開不完的會和應付不完的客戶,
另外還須與主管、部下或同事等相處。
辦公室的人際關係不僅需要體力也要腦力,
因此可實際應用之溝通句型及表達方式就
相當地多。

Words 單字篇

㉕客戶；顧客

❺分機
❻外線
❸電話
❹電話聽筒
❾螢光筆
❽自動鉛筆
㉖名片

⓫收據
⓬帳單；發票
⓾便條紙簿
❼計算機

⓭抽屜

⓯辦公室用品

⓮旋轉椅

❶time recorder ❷ID card ❸telephone ❹handset ❺extension line ❻external line ❼calculator ❽mechanical pencil ❾marker ⓾memo pad ⓫receipt ⓬bill/invoice ⓭drawer ⓮swivel chair

首先，讓我們透過各種物品的名稱，
來掌握「辦公室工作」給人的整體印象。

⑯資料
⑱佈告欄
㉒老闆
㉓員工
㉔文件
⑰檔案櫃
⑲影印機
⑳傳真機
❶打卡鐘
❷識別證
㉑設備；器材

⑮office supplies　⑯material　⑰file cabinet　⑱bulletin board
⑲copier　⑳fax machine　㉑equipment　㉒boss　㉓staff
㉔document　㉕client /customer　㉖business card

1　我把識別卡刷過打卡鐘。
I swipe my ID card through a time recorder.

2　我打開置物櫃，把包包放進去。
I open the locker and put my bag in.

3　我接電話。
I answer the phone.

4　我記筆記。
I take notes.

5　我轉一通電話。
I transfer a phone call.

tips

❶ swipe A through B 就是「把 A 刷過 B」之意，而「可讀取或刷磁卡的機器」就統稱為 card swipe [device]。
❸ 在一般會話中也可用 get the phone（接電話）。
❹「記下～」可說成 get down ~ 或 jot down ~。
❻「請您稍候不要掛電話」說成 Would you <u>hold on</u> / <u>hold the</u>

6 我掛電話。
I hang up [the phone].

7 我留言給別人。
I give someone a message.

8 我把外線電話和內線分機搞混了。
I mix up an external line with an extension line.

9 我打電話前先撥 0。
I dial 0 first before making a phone call.

10 我使用計算機計算。
I use a calculator.

line, please? 。
❼「是否需要幫您留個言？」說成 Would you like to leave a message? 。
❽ mix up A with B 是指「把 A 和 B 搞混了」。
❿ 也可說成 I work with a calculator. 。

11 我提交文件。
I submit the documents.

12 我在文件上蓋章。
I stamp the documents.

13 我整理我的資料。
I organize my material.

14 我影印一些東西。
I make some copies.

15 我準備一些資料並分發影本。
I prepare some material and distribute copies.

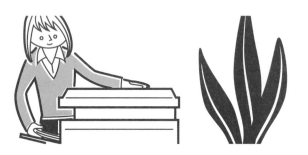

tips

❶ 「提交～」也可用 turn in ～ 或 hand in ～。
❷ 文件也可說成 papers（複數形）。
❸ 「整理桌面；收拾桌面」說成 tidy up the desk。
❹ 「影印」也可說成 <u>make photocopies</u> / <u>xerox copies</u>（Xerox 原指「全錄」，為商標名）。
❺ 「起草〔文件等〕」說成 draw up ～。

16 我用傳真（電子郵件）傳送一份文件。
I send a document by fax (e-mail).

17 我用碎紙機絞碎一份文件。
I shred a document.

18 我把收據送到會計部門。
I pass my receipt on to the accounting department.

19 我核銷費用。
I get reimbursed for my expenses.

20 他們把信件遞送到公司的每一個單位。
They deliver mail throughout the company.

⓱ shred 作名詞用時指「細長的碎片」。
⓲ 收據憑單可說成 voucher，例如 travel voucher（〔出差等的〕旅費收據）。
⓳ reimburse 指「報帳並獲得～的補貼」，即「報銷～費用」之意，而 reimburse（人）for ～ 就是指「給（人）～費用的補貼」。
⓴ 若要表達「傳閱〔文件等〕」之意時，就用 circulate，例如 They circulate the memo.（他們傳閱公司備忘錄）。

chapter ④ Working at the Office

21 我整理我的桌面。
I organize the top of my desk.

22 我們傳閱一份簽呈。
We circulate a petition.

23 我和我的屬下有個會要開。
I have a meeting with my staff.

24 我出席一場會議。
I attend a meeting.

25 我在會議上發言。
I speak at the meeting.

tips

㉑ organize 就是「整理～」之意，而 clean 是「清潔～」之意。

㉒ petition 一般指「請願書」或「訴狀」。

㉓ 「屬下」的正式說法是 subordinate，相反的「上司」就是 superior。不過一般常用 boss 來指稱上司，用 staff 來指稱屬下。

26 我準備簡報。
I prepare for my presentation.

27 我預約會議室。
I book a room for the meeting.

28 我們和海外客戶進行視訊會議。
We hold a videoconference with clients overseas.

29 我與客戶會面。
I meet a client.

30 我和客戶交換名片。
I exchange business cards with a client.

㉖ 「進行簡報」可說成 <u>make/do</u> a presentation。
㉗ book 為動詞，表示「預約～」之意。
㉘ 此句也可使用 We talk via videoconference with ～ 這樣的句型。

31 我四處推銷產品。
I make the rounds to sell the product.

32 我去出〔一天的〕差。
I go on a [one-day] business trip.

33 我們行銷我們的商品。
We market our merchandise.

34 我們招待客戶。
We entertain our customers.

35 我直接去〔現場〕。
I go directly [to the site].

㉜ 「出差」在職場上常說成 go out of town。另外也可用 travel 這個字，例如 I travel three days a week on business.（我每週出差 3 天）。

㉞ customer 主要指「購買產品的顧客」，而 client 則是「有業務往來的客戶」。

36 我午休。
I take a lunch break.

37 我補妝。
I redo my makeup.

38 我比我的前輩更早獲得升遷。
I get promoted ahead of my senior.

39 我因為業績優秀而獲得表揚。
I am commended for achieving excellent sales results.

40 我收到正式的調職通知。
I receive an official notification of appointment to transfer.

㊱「出去吃午飯」説成 go out for lunch，而「因吃午飯而外出」則説成 be out to lunch。

㊳「升官；晉升」也可説成 <u>get</u>/ <u>receive</u> a promotion。

1 這裡的企業文化著眼於促進開放式溝通。
The corporate culture here is one that fosters open communication.

2 我的工作堆積如山。
My work has been piling up.

3 我的工作進度不如預期。
My work is not progressing as much as I'd hoped.

4 首先，我應該要設定事情的優先順序。
First, I should set priorities for what to do.

5 不知為何，我今天腦袋不清楚。
I don't know why but my head is fuzzy today.

6 老闆今天不在。咱們輕鬆一下！
The boss is out today. Let's relax!

corporate culture = 企業文化／foster = 培養；促進

「公司風氣」可說成 corporate <u>atmosphere</u>/<u>character</u>。另外「企業的透明度」則是 corporate clarity，例如 Our company focuses on corporate clarity.（我們公司很重視企業的透明度）。

---

pile up ＝累積

「一堆文件」就說成 a <u>pile</u>/<u>heap</u>/<u>stack</u> of documents，例如 First, I should begin with this pile of documents.（首先，我該從這堆文件下手）。

---

progress = 進展；進行／as much as ～ = 與～相同程度

progress 做為名詞時表示「進度」，例如「專案進度如何？」就可說成 What's the progress on the project?。不過，也可不用 progress這個字，而說成 How's the project coming along?

---

set priorities for ～ = 替～設定優先順序

碰到做事先後順序不明確、個性優柔寡斷的人時，可以建議他 Get your priorities straight.（請先搞清楚事情的優先順序吧）。

---

fuzzy = 模糊的；不清楚的

「我的腦袋不清楚」也可說成 I have a stuffy head. 或 My head isn't clear today.。另外還有 My brain is out to lunch.（我的腦袋去吃午飯了）這種講法。

---

be out = 外出中／relax = 放鬆

「山中無老虎，猴子稱大王」以英語來表達就是 When the cat's away, the mice will play.（貓咪不在，老鼠作亂）。

7 怎麼能用那麼多的時間做這麼簡單的工作？

How can you spend so much time doing such a simple task?

8 你已經不是新進員工了，到現在應該要知道該怎麼做了。

You're not a new recruit any more so you should know how to do it by now.

9 他這麼小心謹慎地工作是好事，但……。

The fact that he does his job carefully is a good thing, but ...

10 我現在正忙得不可開交。你可以等一下嗎？

I'm tied up right now. Would you ask me later?

11 別這麼大聲講電話，整個樓層的人都聽得見你的聲音。

Don't talk over the phone in such a loud voice that everyone on the floor can hear you.

12 你一點安排計劃的概念都沒有。

You have no sense of scheduling.

How can you ~ ? = 你怎麼能～？／task = 工作；任務

How can you ~ ? 這種句型依情況不同，可能表示憤怒，也可能表示不耐煩。而 spend +（時間）+ -ing 可表達「花費（時間）做～」，例如 We spent two hours discussing the project.（我們花了 2 小時討論該專案）。

[new] recruit = 新進員工／how to do ~ = ～該怎麼做／by now = 到現在

「覺得受夠了」這種情緒可用 You never give me a break.（你還真是讓我一刻也不得閒）或 Quit wasting my time.（別再浪費我的時間了）等說法來表達。

---

carefully = 仔細地／a good thing = 好事

The fact that S + V is ~ 這種句型可用來表示「S 做 V 這件事算是～」之意。而此例句也可改用 It is ~ that S + V 之句型，說成 It is a good thing that he does his job carefully, but ...。

---

be tied up = 脫不了身；忙得不可開交／right now = 現在；眼前

be tied up 之後經常會接著忙碌的理由或地點，例如 I'm tied up with replying to e-mail now.（我正忙著回電子郵件）或 We were tied up in a meeting all morning.（我們整個早上都忙著開會）等。

---

over the phone = 用電話；透過電話

這句話可以說成 Don't talk over the phone in such a loud voice that carries throughout the floor. 另外，也可以說 Please be quiet here. Sound carries.（在此請保持安靜。聲音會傳得很遠）。

---

sense = 感覺；概念

a sense of ~ 表示「對～的概念；～感」，而 no sense of ~ 便是相反的意思。此句也可說成 You don't manage time very well.（你時間管理得不太好）。

13 噢，我的天啊！我有兩個約會撞期了。

Oh, my gosh! I've got two appointments double-booked.

14 我得做一場英語簡報。好緊張。

I have a presentation to make in English. I'm so nervous.

15 我想我應該會是本月份的業績冠軍吧。

I think I'll be top in the sales performance ranking for this month.

16 聽說史密斯先生拿到了一筆大訂單。

They say Mr. Smith got a big contract.

17 文書工作總令我肩頸僵硬。

Desk work definitely gives me a stiff neck.

18 使用電腦造成我的眼睛乾燥。

Working on a computer makes my eyes dry.

get ~ double-booked = 重複預訂～／appointment = 預約；約會

<u>Oh, my gosh!/Gosh!</u> 是 <u>Oh, my god!/God!</u> 較委婉的講法，用來表達吃驚或不愉快的感覺。也可以用 Oh, my goodness! 由於動不動就直呼神（God）之名會被認為不夠尊敬，所以大家偏好使用 gosh 或 goodness。

- -

presentation = 簡報；發表／nervous = 緊張的

可用來表達「緊張狀態」的説法還有 get butterflies in one's stomach（忐忑不安）、get cold feet（〔緊張得〕臨陣退縮）、on the edge of one's chair（焦躁不安）等等。

- -

sales performance = 銷售業績／ranking = 排名

「我因業績優秀而獲得特別獎金」可説成 I am awarded a special bonus for superior sales performance.。另外，「業務員；業務代表」則是 sales <u>rep</u>/<u>representative</u>。

- -

contract = 合約 e.g. sign a contract = 簽訂合約

- -

desk work =〔坐在辦公桌前做的〕文書工作／definitely = 明確地；肯定地／stiff neck = 肩頸僵硬

「肩頸僵硬」也可説成 stiff shoulders，但是由於實際僵硬的部分多為脖子而非肩膀，因此較常使用 neck。另，feel stiff around the neck、feel tense around the neck 等也具有同樣的意思。

- -

work on ~ = 用～工作

「一直盯著電腦螢幕看，造成我的眼睛疲勞」可説成 I get eye strain from staring at the computer screen.。「我每隔 2 小時滴一次眼藥水」則説成 I apply eye drops every two hours.。

19 好冷（熱）！冷氣（暖氣）是不是開得太強了點？
It's cold (hot) in here. Isn't the air conditioner (heat) a little too strong?

20 傳真機又卡紙了。
The fax machine paper got jammed again.

21 這份文件必須印成彩色的。
This document has to be printed in color.

22 我不知道我們收到了傳真的未送達通知。
I didn't know we'd received a non-delivery notice.

23 抱歉，長官。這跟您前幾天告訴我們的好像不太一樣？
Excuse me, sir. Isn't it a bit different from what you told us the other day?

24 他剛剛的發言有點太接近性騷擾了，不是嗎？
What he just said is a little too close to sexual harassment, isn't it?

air conditioner = 空調；冷氣

「他們為何每天都把冷氣開得那麼強？」説成 Why do they crank up the air conditioner every day?。「我們工作時都把冷氣開到很大」則可以説 We work with air-conditioner blasting.。

---

get jammed =〔紙張等〕卡住了

jammed 為形容詞，意思是「卡住的」，也可以指「塞滿的」、「擁擠的」例如 The street is jammed with cars.（街道上塞滿了汽車）、The show is jammed with people.（這場表演擠滿了人）等。

---

document = 文件／in color = 以彩色的方式

「以黑白的方式」就是 in black and white，例如 We should print materials in black and white since it costs less.（我們應該將資料印成黑白的，因為成本較低）。

---

receive = 接收～／non-delivery notice = 未送達通知

we'd 是 we had 的縮寫。因為收到傳真發生在「過去的過去」，所以用過去完成式。

---

a bit = 有點；有些／different from ~ = 和～不同／the other day = 前幾天

一般來説，在美國稱地位高於自己的男性 Sir，女性 Ma'am。

---

close to ~ = 很接近～／sexual harassment = 性騷擾

若想對同事表達「對於性別歧視的言論，你應該更注意一點比較好」之意，可以説成 You should be more sensitive about sexually discriminating statements.。此句中的 discriminating 是「歧視的」之意。

25 我對老闆唯命是從。
I'm at the boss's beck and call.

26 我會去跟我的上司商量看看。
I'll go have a little talk with my boss.

27 每次需要主任時，他總是不在！
The chief is never in when he's needed!

28 他們現在要我加班？我晚上有事。
They're asking me to work overtime now? I have plans for tonight.

29 我每天加班都沒有加班費。
I work overtime without pay every day.

30 看在錢的份上，讓我們開始認真工作吧。
Let's just think about the money and get down to work.

be at someone's beck and call = 聽從某人的使喚／beck = 招手／call = 叫喚

而「受～的擺佈」可説成 be under someone's thumb，如 Mr. Farmer is under his boss's thumb.（法默先生受他老闆的擺佈）。另外，「馬屁精」就是 brown-noser，例如 Bill is a brown-noser.（比爾是個馬屁精／比爾很狗腿）。

---

go have = go and have（go 或 come 之後的 and 經常會被省略）／have a talk with ～ = 和～商量；和～談談

「和～談談」也可用 have a word，例如 May I have a word with you?（我可以跟你談談嗎？）。而 have words with ～ 則是「與～爭論」之意，請特別注意。

---

chief =主任／be in = 在〔辦公室、公司等〕

在電話中欲表達「莊先生／小姐目前不在座位上」時，就説成 I'm sorry, Mr./Ms. Chuang is not at his/her desk.。而「莊先生／小姐今天請病假」則説成 Mr./Ms. Chuang is off sick today.。

---

ask ～ to ... = 要求～做……／work overtime = 加班；超時工作

work overtime 指「加班」，與 overwork（過勞）不一樣，請特別注意。另外，「加班費」可説成 overtime allowance。

---

without pay = 無酬勞的；無薪的

「加班沒有加班費」也可以説成 be not paid extra for overtime.。

---

get down to ～ = 開始認真～

在職場閒聊（small talk）結束後，想表達「那麼，讓我們言歸正傳」的意思時，可説成 Let's get down to business. 或 Let's get down to brass tacks. 等。第二句話中的 brass tacks 原意為「黃銅製的圖釘」，後來則衍伸為「基本事實；核心要點」之意。

31 這個可以報帳嗎？
Can we put this down to expenses?

32 我好睏。可能是因為午餐吃太飽了。
I'm feeling drowsy. Maybe because I had a heavy lunch.

33 我還有 3 天的有薪假。
I have three more paid holidays.

34 我的妝在傍晚前就差不多都掉了。
My makeup wears off by evening.

35 咱們今天試試看能不能準時下班。
Let's try and leave the office on time today.

36 你何不停止思考辭職的事，堅守目前的工作崗位就好？
Why don't you stop thinking about quitting and just stick to your current job?

put ~ down to expenses = 將～納入支出費用；將～拿來報帳 cf. reduce/cut down on expenses = 減少開支／pad an expense account = 浮報費用／be on the company = 算成公司的費用；報公帳

---

drowsy = 昏昏欲睡的／heavy lunch = 大份量的午餐

drowsy 這個形容詞可表達比 sleepy（想睡的）更強烈的睡意。例如 I always get drowsy after lunch.（我吃完午飯後總是昏昏欲睡）。drowsy的名詞為 drowsiness，用法如 The afternoon meeting induces drowsiness.（下午的會議總能引發強烈睡意）。

---

paid holiday = 有薪休假

「有薪休假」相關的用法還有 carry over unused paid holidays（將未使用的有薪休假展延〔至下一年度〕）、use up one's paid holidays（消化有薪休假）等。

---

wear off = 漸漸掉光；逐漸消逝／by evening = 在傍晚前

此例句也可改成 My makeup comes off by evening.。而「補妝」則說成 fix/redo one's makeup，「卸妝」說成 take off one's makeup。

---

leave the office = 下班；離開辦公室回家／on time = 準時

以每天固定的作息來說，「準時」說成 on time（e.g. I come in on time. 我準時上班），而「及時趕上」特殊活動則用 in time（e.g. I made it in time for the show. 我及時趕上那場表演）。

---

stop -ing = 停止～／quit = 辭職／stick to ~ = 堅守～；忠於～／current job = 目前的工作

Why don't you ~? 表示「何不做～呢？」，可用於以輕鬆態度向對方提出忠告的時候。另外，How about ~? 或 What about ~? 則有「提出簡單建議」的意思。

性騷擾的防範對策、 會議前的準備工作等常是辦公室
對話的主題

Woman1: I can't believe John said your skirt is too short.

Woman2: It's a little too close to sexual harassment, isn't it?

W1: Yes, it is. Besides❶, your skirt's not that short❷.

W2: Why did he have to say that today? I have a presentation to make in English. I'm so nervous.

W1: Have you organized your material?

W2: Yes, I did it all yesterday. I prepared my materials and I'm going to distribute copies.

W1: Is there anything I can do to help?

W2: Actually❸, this document has to be printed in color. Could you make 20 copies?

W1: No problem❹. I have to attend a meeting at four, but there's plenty of❺ time before that.

W2: Where is the meeting?

W1: Oh, I have to book a room for the meeting. Thanks for reminding❻ me.

W2: I still don't like what John said. I think I'll go have a little talk with my boss.

W1: I'm sure he'll be able to help. Say❼, let's try and leave the office on time today. I'd like to go out for a drink❽.

W2: OK! I work overtime without pay every day. I think I deserve❾ a drink after today!

女子 1：我真不敢相信約翰竟然說妳的裙子太短。

女子 2：這話有點太接近性騷擾了，不是嗎？

女 1：是的，沒錯。而且妳的裙子也沒那麼短呀。

女 2：他為什麼非要挑今天講這種話？我剛好得做一場英語簡報。我好緊張。

女 1：資料都整理好了嗎？

女 2：好了，我昨天都整理好了。我準備了資料，要分發影本給大家。

女 1：有什麼我可以幫忙的嗎？

女 2：事實上，這份文件必須印成彩色的。妳可以幫忙印 20 份嗎？

女 1：沒問題。我 4 點必須參加一個會議，不過在那之前還有很充足的時間。

女 2：妳的會議在哪裡開？

女 1：噢，我得預約會議室才行。謝謝妳提醒我。

女 2：我還是很不喜歡約翰說的話。我想我會去跟我老闆談一談。

女 1：我想他一定能幫上忙的。對了，咱們今天試試看能不能準時下班。我想去喝一杯。

女 2：OK！我每天加班都沒有加班費。我想今天下班後我應該可以去喝一杯。

【單字片語】

❶ besides：此外；而且
❷ not that short：沒那麼短
❸ actually：事實上
❹ No problem.：沒問題
❺ plenty of～：充足的～
❻ remind：提醒
❼ say：對了
❽ go out for a drink：去喝一杯
❾ deserve：應得～

Quick Check

讓我們一起來複習本章所介紹過的句型！請依據以下中文句子的意思，來完成對應的英文句子。（答案就在本頁最下方。）

❶ 我把識別卡刷過打卡鐘。 →P096
I ( ) my ID card ( ) a time recorder.

❷ 我們和海外客戶進行視訊會議。 →P100
We ( ) a ( ) with ( ) overseas.

❸ 我四處推銷產品。 →P102
I ( ) ( ) ( ) to sell the product.

❹ 我比我的前輩更早獲得升遷。 →P103
I ( ) ( ) ( ) ( ) my senior.

❺ 這裡的企業文化著眼於促進開放式溝通。 →P104
The ( ) ( ) here is one that ( ) open ( ).

❻ 我現在正忙得不可開交。你可以等一下嗎？ →P106
( ) ( ) ( ) right now. Would you ask me
( )?

❼ 噢，我的天啊！我有兩個約會撞期了。 →P108
Oh, my gosh! I've ( ) two ( ) ( ).

❽ 我對老闆唯命是從。 →P112
I'm ( ) ( ) boss's ( ) ( ) ( ).

❾ 這個可以報帳嗎？ →P114
Can we ( ) this ( ) ( ) ( )?

❿ 我還有 3 天的有薪假。 →P114
I ( ) three ( ) ( ) ( ).

---

❶ swipe/through ❷ hold/videoconference/clients ❸ make/the/rounds ❹ get/promoted/ahead/of ❺ corporate/culture/fosters/communication ❻ I'm/tied/up/later ❼ got/appointments/double-booked ❽ at/the/beck/and/call ❾ put/down/to/expenses ❿ have/more/paid/holidays

chapter 5

The IT Life

資訊生活

近年來，與資訊科技相關的字詞遽增。
各種年齡的人們都會在日常生活中，
使用手機交談、相互寄送電子郵件、
上網查詢各式資訊，也撰寫部落格文章，
資訊科技已深入現代生活中。

Words 單字篇

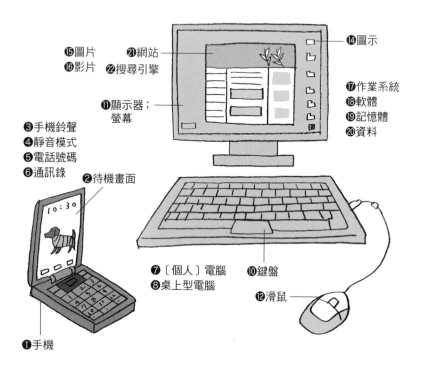

⑮圖片　㉑網站
⑯影片　㉒搜尋引擎

⑭圖示

⑰作業系統
⑱軟體
⑲記憶體
⑳資料

⑪顯示器；螢幕

③手機鈴聲
④靜音模式
⑤電話號碼
⑥通訊錄

②待機畫面

⑦〔個人〕電腦
⑧桌上型電腦

⑩鍵盤

⑫滑鼠

①手機

❶ cellphone　❷ stand-by screen　❸ ringtone　❹ silent mode
❺ phone number　❻ address list　❼ [personal] computer　❽ desktop
computer　❾ laptop　❿ keyboard　⓫ monitor　⓬ mouse　⓭ USB flash

首先，讓我們透過各種物品的名稱，
來掌握「資訊生活」給人的整體印象。

❾筆記型電腦

㉓電子郵件
㉔附檔；附件
㉕垃圾郵件

⓭ USB 隨身碟

drive ⓮ icon ⓯ picture ⓰ video ⓱ OS(operating system)
⓲ software ⓳ memory ⓴ data ㉑ website ㉒ search engine
㉓ e-mail ㉔ attached file ㉕ junk mail

1　我換用不同機種的手機。
I replace my cellphone with another model.

2　我用手機拍照並寄出。
I take a photo on my cellphone camera and send it.

3　我下載手機鈴聲。
I download a ringtone melody.

4　我把手機設成靜音模式。
I set my cellphone to silent mode.

5　我替手機充電。
I recharge my cellphone.

tips

❶ replace A with B 是指「用 B 取代 A」。另，cellphone 也可說成 mobile phone。

❸ 這是由 ring（電話鈴聲）+ tone（音調）所形成的單字，而「歌曲」類的鈴聲也算是 ringtone。

❹ Please set your mobile phone to silent mode and refrain

6 我更改手機的桌面。
**I change the wallpaper
on my cellphone.**

7 我用紅外線功能交換地址與電話號碼。
**I exchange addresses and phone numbers
with the infrared function.**

8 我將電腦開機。
**I start up
my computer.**

9 我重新啟動電腦。
**I reboot
my computer.**

10 我做備份。
I make a backup copy.

from talking on the phone.（請將您的手機設定為靜音模式，並且盡量不要講電話）。

❻ 「桌面」即「待機畫面」，因此也可說成 idle screen、stand-by display。

❽ 「〔電腦〕開機」也可使用 boot 這個動詞。

11 我安裝軟體。
I install the software.

12 我升級軟體。
I upgrade the software.

13 我替電腦增加更多記憶體。
I add more memory to my computer.

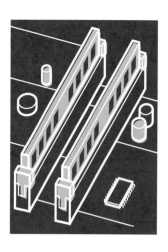

14 我把印表機接到電腦上。
I connect the printer to the computer.

15 我把文件列印出來。
I print out the document.

tips

⓫ software 是不可數名詞，所以不用複數形。
⓰ 「〔將磁碟機等〕初始化；格式化」則要使用 format 這個字。
⓱ OS 就是 operating system（作業系統）的縮寫，是電腦中最基本的軟體。

16 我將電腦初始化。
I initialize the computer.

17 我升級作業系統。
I update the OS software.

18 我連續按兩次那個圖示。
I double-click on the icon.

19 我拖放那個圖示。
I drag-and-drop the icon.

20 我更改電腦的桌面背景。
I change the wallpaper on my computer.

⓲ 「連按兩下」也可說成 click twice。
⓳ 所謂的拖放操作，就是用滑鼠把檔案圖示等拖拉移動（drag）至另一處後，再放開（drop）。

21 我把照片掃描進電腦裡。
I scan a picture into my computer.

22 我的電腦中毒了。
My PC gets infected with a computer virus.

23 我把資料存在 USB 隨身碟裡。
I save the data on my USB flash drive.

24 我壓縮一個檔案。
I compress a file.

25 我註冊登錄一家網路服務供應商。
I sign up with an Internet service provider.

tips

㉒ 「我清除電腦裡的病毒」就說成 I rid the computer of the virus.。

㉓ USB 是 Universal Serial Bus 的縮寫。在會話中有時也將 USB隨身碟說成 memory stick。

㉔ 「我把檔案解壓縮」說成 I <u>decompress</u>/<u>unzip</u> the file.。

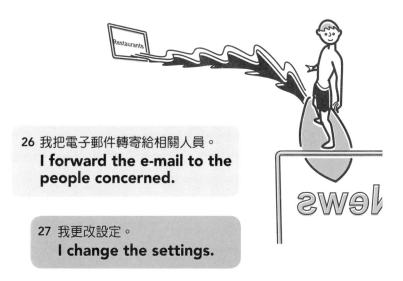

26 我把電子郵件轉寄給相關人員。
I forward the e-mail to the people concerned.

27 我更改設定。
I change the settings.

28 我製作自己的網站。
I create my own website.

29 我瀏覽網路。
I browse the Internet.

30 我把網站加入書籤（我的最愛）中。
I bookmark the site.

㉕ 一般來說「註冊登錄～」用 sign up with ~，「申請～〔服務等〕」則用 subscribe to ~，而「與～簽訂契約」就用 contract with ~。
㉖ 這裡的 concerned 是放在名詞之後，用來修飾該名詞的形容詞。
㉙ browse 也有「〔在書店等地方〕隨意翻閱」之意。另外「逛網站」可說成 surf websites 或 surf the Internet。
㉚ 這句也可說成 I have the site bookmarked.。

31 我在網路上聊天。
I have a chat on the Internet.

32 我用搜尋引擎尋找一些網站。
I look for some websites with the search engine.

33 我在部落格上提供連結。
I provide a link on my blog.

34 我在網路上查閱東西。
I do some research on the Internet.

35 我在線上討論區中張貼訊息。
I post a message on an online discussion board.

tips

㉛ 這句也可說成 I chat on the Internet.。

㉜ 最具代表性的搜尋引擎 Google 已可做為動詞直接使用,例如 I Google/ do a Google search for the word.(我用 Google 搜尋那個字)。

㊱ blog 是用 web(網路)+ log(日誌)所造出的字。

36 我推出自己的部落格。
I launch my own blog.

37 我在 po 出的文章中放上連往
另一個部落格的引用連結。
**I put a trackback link to
another blog in my post.**

38 我回覆訊息。
I respond to a message.

39 我用電子郵件傳送附檔。
I send an e-mail attachment.

40 我開啟附檔。
I open an attached file.

㊲ 部落格引用（trackback）功能的運作方式，可用英文説明為 My blog automatically notifies another blog about my new entry and a link to my entry will appear in that blog.（當我的部落格有新文章時，就會自動通知另一個部落格，而連往我文章的連結會出現在該部落格中）。

1 手機的資費方案很難理解。
Cellphone rate plans are hard to understand.

2 我知道這支手機具有各式各樣的功能，但是我無法充分利用。
I know this cellphone has various functions, but I can't make full use of them.

3 我的手機現在沒訊號，因為我在地下室。
My cellphone is out of service now because I'm in the basement.

4 近來，手機不論在哪兒收訊都很好。
Cellphones can get good reception anywhere these days.

5 只要是能讓我可以打電話和寄電子郵件，任何手機都行。
Any cellphone will do, as long as I can make calls and send e-mail.

6 當我的手機鈴聲在會議中響起時，真令我尷尬。
I was embarrassed when my ringtone sounded during the meeting.

cellphone (= <u>cellular telephone</u> / <u>mobile telephone</u>) = 手機／rate = 費率；
價格

hard to understand 就是 confusing（令人困惑的）、complicated（複雜
的），故此例句也可改為 Cellphone rate plans are <u>confusing</u> / <u>complicated</u>。

---

various = 各式各樣的／function = 功能／make full use of ~ = 充分利用~

make use of ~ 即「利用~」之意，而在 use 之前可以加上不同形容詞，例如
make <u>good</u> use of ~（好好利用~），make <u>best</u> use of ~（將~做最好的運
用），make <u>bad</u> use of ~（將~用在不好的地方；濫用~）等。

---

out of service = 在服務範圍之外；收不到訊號／basement = 地下室

「〔手機〕在服務範圍外」也可說成 out of range，例如 Most cellphones
used to go out of range in the subway.（以前大部分手機在地鐵裡都收不到訊
號）。

---

reception =〔訊號的〕接收狀況／anywhere = 到處；任何地方／these days =
近來

reception 是動詞 receive（接收~）的名詞形，代表「接收訊號」之意。The
reception level should be very good because there're three bars showing on
the screen.（訊號的接收度應該非常好，因為螢幕上顯示了 3 格）。

---

do = 可行；可用／as long as ~ = 只要~／make a call = 打電話

本句中的 will 可換成 can。

---

be embarrassed = 丟臉的；尷尬的／ringtone = 手機鈴聲；來電鈴聲

英語中，相當於「〔太過丟臉以至於〕想挖個地洞鑽進去」的說法是 I could
have crawled under the rug.（我當時真想鑽到地毯下去）。

7 我弄丟了手機！通訊錄也跟著沒了。

I've lost my cellphone! My address list is gone as well.

---

8 那對情侶是怎麼了？約會時怎麼老是各自盯著自己的手機看。

What is it with that couple? Each staring at their own cellphone all the time on a date.

---

9 我沒有使用無限上網方案，卻看了好多影片。

I watched a lot of videos without using the unlimited download package.

---

10 這個軟體和我舊的作業系統相容嗎？

Is this software compatible with my old OS?

---

11 這和 Mac 不相容，對吧？

That's not Mac-compatible, is it?

---

12 我知道有新的作業系統上市了，但是我們還是先觀望一下再看是否該買。

I know a new OS is hitting the market, but let's wait and see if I should buy it.

be gone = 走掉了；不見了／as well = 也；同樣地

此例句的後半句也可說成 My address list was ruined.（我的通訊錄毀了）、 My address list went down the drain.（我的通訊錄成了泡影）等。 go down the drain 直譯成中文是「流入排水管」。

---

stare at ~ = 盯著~看／on a date = 在約會中

What is it with ~ ? 是「~是怎麼了？；~是怎麼回事？」之意。 What is it with you? 就是「你怎麼了？」。而 What's up with ~?（~是什麼樣的情況？）也可表達類似意思。

---

unlimited download package = 無限上網方案；上網吃到飽專案

「無限的；吃到飽」也可說成 unmetered，例如 The cellphone carrier offers unmetered downloads for Internet games.（這間手機公司提供網路遊戲無限下載的服務）。

---

be compatible with ~ = 和~相容

反之，「和~不相容」就說成 be incompatible with ~，例如 Unfortunately, the software is incompatible with my computer.（很不幸，這軟體和我的電腦不相容）。

~-compatible = 和~相容的

「相容性」就叫 compatibility，例如 This software doesn't work well on my computer due to a compatibility problem.（由於有相容性問題，因此這軟體在我電腦上無法運作）。

---

hit the <u>market</u>/<u>marketplace</u> = 上市／wait and see if ~ = 先觀望再看是否要~

使用 market（市場）一詞的類似說法還有 go on the market，例如 The new product will go on the market in April.（此新產品將於 4 月份上市）。

13 這電腦讓我很洩氣，因為它開機實在很慢。
The computer makes me frustrated because it takes so long to boot.

14 它一直當機！
It keeps freezing!

15 我的電腦一播影片就會自動關機。
My computer automatically shuts down the moment I play a video.

16 這個觸控螢幕不夠靈敏。
This touchscreen is not sensitive enough.

17 你同時執行太多軟體了。
You're running too much software at once.

18 安裝防毒軟體後，我的電腦就變慢了。
My computer became slower after installing anti-virus software.

make ~ frustrated = 令～感到灰心／boot =〔機器之類的〕開機

欲強調「需花很長時間」，可使用 forever（永遠）來表達，例如 It takes forever to boot.（它開機要花非常久的時間）。

---

keep -ing = 一直～／freeze =〔電腦〕當機；停住不動

這句也可說成 It's frozen again!，不過原例句較能強調「總是一直～」的意思。另，「當機」也可用crash，例如 My computer crashed.（我的電腦當機了。）

---

shut down =〔電腦的〕電源關閉；關機／the moment ~ = 做～的那一剎那

注意，the moment S + V 中的 the moment 為連接詞的用法，可改為 ... as soon as...。

---

touchscreen = 觸控螢幕／sensitive = 靈敏的；敏感的

sensitive 有「能感應的」之意，如 This screen is touch-sensitive.（這個螢幕能感應觸碰）。

---

run ~ = 執行～；啟動～／software = 軟體（不可數名詞）／at once = 同時

將過去分詞的 run 接在名詞之後，就變成形容詞，意思為「靠～運作的」。例如 battery-run laptop（靠電池運作的筆記型電腦）。而 ~-driven（靠～驅動的）也具有類似意義，例如 motor-driven vehicle（靠馬達驅動的車輛）。

---

install = 安裝／anti-virus software = 防毒軟體

install原意就是「設置～；安裝～」，例如 A new air-conditioner will be installed in our office this week.（本週，我們辦公室將安裝一台新的空調）。

19 我希望裝了這個以後不會再出現軟體失靈的情況。
I hope there'll be no software glitches after installing this.

20 天呀！我的電腦已經沒有任何剩餘空間了嗎？！
Gee! Isn't there any space left on my computer?!

21 增加了記憶體後，我的電腦就運作得很順暢。
With additional memory my computer runs very smoothly.

22 近來，我可以馬上輸入並搜尋任何我想查的東西。真方便！
These days, I can type in anything I wish to search for right away. How convenient!

23 就算在透過網路搜尋釐清了我的問題之後，我還是很少會記得答案。
Even after my question has been cleared up by Googling, I seldom remember the answer.

24 在網路上申請比較便宜。
It's cheaper if you apply online.

glitch =〔機器的〕失靈;小故障

glitch 也有「〔計畫等的〕缺點;差錯」之意,例如 There was a small glitch with the shipment and I haven't received my order yet.(貨運部分出了點小差錯,我還沒收到我訂的東西)。

Gee! = 天啊!leave = 剩下

Gee! 是用來表達「哎呀;糟糕」等驚訝或失望之意的感嘆詞。由於 Jesus! 及 God! 等都是很強烈的用字,故用發音近似的 Gee! 來代替。

---

additional = 添加的/run =〔程式等〕執行;運作/smoothly = 順暢地;流暢地

with 是用來表示「有了~」之意的介系詞,例如 With this laptop, I can check my e-mail anywhere.(有了這台筆記型電腦,我就能隨時隨地接收電子郵件)。

---

wish to ~ = 想要~/right away = 立刻/convenient = 方便的

wish 後若接名詞子句,表達的是現實生活中不可能實現的願望(e.g. I wish I were a native speaker of English.);若接不定詞,表達的就是單純的「想要~」之意(e.g. I wish to learn English.)。

---

clear ~ up = 釐清~/Google(動詞)=〔使用 Google〕搜尋/seldom = 很少

Google 是著名的搜尋引擎公司名,最近已被動詞化成一般用字,因此有時會將第一個字母寫成小寫(google),例如 Why don't you google it on your PC?(你何不用你的電腦搜尋看看?)。

---

apply = 申請/online = 網上;線上

online 可做形容詞用,例如 online shopping(網路購物),也可作副詞用,例如 buy (order) online(在網上購物(訂購))。

25 哇！我最喜歡的樂團有新影片上傳到 YouTube 了！
Wow! A new video from my favorite band has been uploaded onto YouTube!

26 要維持社群網路上的人際關係可真辛苦。
Keeping up the relationships on social networking services is a pain.

27 我又在臉書上遇到一個老朋友。
I met an old friend of mine again on Facebook.

28 我和在網路上認識的人見面，但是他和我想像的完全不同。
I met a guy I got to know on the Net, but he was completely different than what I'd imagined.

29 這或許能成為不錯的部落格文章。
This might be a good blog entry.

30 這個部落格正陷入筆戰中。
This blog is in a flame war.

video＝影片／upload ～ onto...＝將～上傳到……　cf. download ～ from the Internet＝從網路下載～

「拍攝影片」説成 shoot videos，「有相機功能的手機」則叫 camera phone 或 camera-equipped cellphone。

---

keep up ～＝維持～／social networking service＝社群網路服務（透過網路來擴大社會關係的服務）／pain＝痛苦；辛苦

pain 這個字的常見用法還有 What a pain!（真麻煩！）、It's a pain in the neck taking three trains there.（去那裡要換兩趟車，真是累人）等。

Facebook＝臉書；FB（世界知名的社群網站之一）

在英文裡，冠詞（a、an、the）和所有格（my、your 等）不能接在一起用，故想表達「我的一個老朋友」時，不能説 a my old friend，而要説成 an old friend of mine。

---

get to know＝認識～

get to ～在會話中經常用來表達「得到做～的機會」之意，例如 If you apply now, you get to try our new product for free.（如果你現在申請，就能獲得免費試用新產品的機會）。

---

blog entry＝部落格的標題、項目、文章

might 為助動詞，表示「有～的可能性」之意。

---

flame war＝〔在網路討論區或部落格文章回覆部分的〕爭論謾罵

此句也可利用及物動詞 flame（〔在網路討論區或個人部落格等處〕猛烈指責），而改成 All the commenters on this blog are flaming each other now.。

31 我連不上那個網站。一定是有一大堆人同時想進入那個網站！

I can't get a connection to the website. There must be a million people trying to access it!

32 這個網站太難更新了。

This site is too difficult to update.

33 主任寄來的電子郵件又是亂碼。

This e-mail from the chief has garbled characters again.

34 我誤開了垃圾郵件。

I've opened some junk mail by mistake.

35 我一個禮拜沒用電腦，所以要回覆這期間累積的所有電子郵件是件很艱鉅的任務。

I didn't use my computer for a week, so it's going to be a big job to answer all the e-mails that piled up meanwhile.

36 這個附檔佔了很大的記憶空間。

This attachment file takes up a lot of memory.

get a connection to ~ = 連結到～／access = 進入；存取〔資料〕

must 為助動詞，代表「一定是～」之意。此例句的後半句也可改成 Definitely a great number of people are accessing it.（肯定有很多人同時在進入）。

---

site (= website) = 網站／update = 更新；提供最新訊息

too ~ to ... 就是「太～以至於無法……」之意。

---

chief = 主任／garble = 使～成亂碼／character = 文字

「變成亂碼的文字」也可説成 funny/weird characters。另外「亂成一團」則可用 jumble、mix up 來表達，例如 The sentences are all jumbled/mixed up.（這些句子都亂成一團了）。

---

junk mail = 垃圾郵件／junk = 垃圾；廢物／by mistake = 錯誤地

「〔以宣傳、廣告為目的之〕垃圾郵件」也可説成 spam [mail/message]。常見的相關用法還有 block spam e-mails（封鎖垃圾郵件）、delete spam messages（刪除垃圾郵件）。此外 spam 還能做為動詞使用，例如 get spammed（收到眾多垃圾郵件）。

---

pile up = 累積／meanwhile = 在該期間

這裡的 big job 指「很辛苦的事」。而若要表示「可真苦了你」等同情之意時，可説成 It's a real/terrible job.。

---

attachment file = 附檔／take up = 佔用〔空間等〕

「附件為～；隨信附上的是～」這類電子商務郵件的用語可利用動詞 attach 來表達，例如 Attached is the itinerary for your trip.（附件為您的旅遊行程説明）。

37 要登記訂閱這免費的電子郵件刊物很容易，但是要取消可就麻煩了。
While it's easy to sign up for this free e-mail publication, it's a real pain to cancel it.

38 糟糕！我把茶灑在鍵盤上了。
Oops! I spilled tea on the keyboard.

與部落格有關的句型

透過部落格抒發心情的人相當多，請利用以下各種表達方式，
試著向全世界發聲吧！

部落客所寫的通知訊息

我開始寫部落格了。 **I've started writing a blog.**

我將寫下我每天的想法與感覺。
I'll be writing what I think and how I feel every day.

通知

結果我的部落格獲選得以出版。
It turns out that my blog has been picked up for publication.

我已決定暫時關閉此部落格。
I've decided to close down this blog for the time being.

sign up for ~ = 登錄～／free e-mail publication = 免費的電子郵件刊物

在會話中，「某事真麻煩」除了可說成 It's a pain. 外，還可以說 What a <u>bother</u>/<u>drag</u>. 等。

Oops! = 糟糕！／spill = 溢出；濺出

Oops!（哎呀！；糟糕！）是在出錯或嚇一跳時發出的感嘆詞。以英語為母語的人都會自然地脫口而出，但是對於非母語人士來說，通常需要特別學習才能用得自然。

平常的問候、一般留言

感謝來訪。　**Thanks for visiting.**

非常感謝大家踴躍回應！
Many thanks for the many comments!

感謝你引用我的文章。
Thanks for trackbacking your blog to mine.

歡迎隨時來訪。　**Please feel free to visit anytime.**

請留下你的意見！　**Please leave some comments!**

我在手機上更新我的部落格。
I'm updating my blog on my cellphone.

我在〔出差〕旅遊時更新了此頁面。
I updated this page during my [business] trip.

我更新得較晚，真是抱歉。　**Sorry for my delayed update.**

很抱歉，我這麼久沒更新我的部落格。
I'm sorry I haven't updated my blog for so long.

○○ 剛好是第 10,000 位訪客。
○○ got the nice round number of 10,000.

也請參觀 ●● 的部落格。
Please visit ●●'s blog, too.

恭喜！你的訪客數達到 10,000 人次了！（訪客留言）
Congrats! You've gotten 10,000 views.

你可自由連結此頁面，但是連結前務必先通知我一聲。
Feel free to link this page to yours, but please let me know before you do.

歡迎引用我的網站。
Trackbacking to my website is always welcome.

新部落格文章請點按此處。
Click here for new blog entries.

本網站正在參與部落格熱門度調查，請點按此處。
This site is participating in a blog popularity survey. Please click here.

請不要故意搗亂或筆戰。 **No trolling or flaming, please.**

未經許可請勿複製轉載。所有著作權皆屬於～所有。
Do not reproduce without permission. All copyright belongs to ~.

平常的問候、一般留言

事務性溝通

警告及禁止說明

我昨天寫的意見因某些理由而被刪除了。
The comment I made yesterday has been deleted for certain reasons.

禁止引用。 **No trackbacking.**

我暫時不接受任何意見回覆。
I will not be accepting any comments for a while.

部落客的自言自語

距離我上次更新部落格已經好一段時間了。
It's been a while since I last updated my blog.

我部落格的訪客人數怎麼還是這麼少？
How come the number of visitors to my blog is still so small?

我該怎麼做才能提升我網站的搜尋引擎排名？
What should I do to raise my search-engine ranking / googlability?

訪客的自言自語

這個部落格真有意思！ **This blog is sooo interesting!**

哇！看這傢伙更新部落格的頻率有多高！
Wow! Look how often this guy updates his blog!

我希望他能多插入些換行。 **I wish he would insert more line feeds.**

這個字型真不利閱讀！ **This font isn't reader-friendly!**

Skit 資訊生活篇

如果你試圖教上一世紀的老古董如何使用電腦⋯⋯

Man1: My computer is making me crazy❶! It keeps freezing up, so I just turned it off❷.

Man2: What OS are you using?

M1: Windows 98. I guess it's a little out of date❸.

M2: A little? You're a dinosaur❹. You need to upgrade your software.

M1: How do I do that?

M2: I'll show you❺. Did you make a backup copy of your documents❻?

M1: Uh ...

M2: Unbelievable. Start up your PC. Now save your data on this USB flash drive. You'd better copy your address book too.

M1: My what?

M2: Were you born yesterday❼? Drag and drop the icon here.

M1: What's an icon?

M2: I'm not even going to answer that. Now put in this CD. Click here to install the software. Then reboot your PC.

M1: My computer wears boots?

M2: Don't be silly. Gee, there isn't any space left. What files do you have on here?

M1: Everything. I haven't deleted anything since I got this computer.

M2: Delete all this old stuff and clear out❽ your e-mail.

M1: Oops! I spilled tea on the keyboard.

M2: I don't know how you survive❾ in this office ... or in this century!

男子 1：我的電腦快讓我抓狂了！它一直停住不動，所以我就把它給關了。

男子 2：你用什麼作業系統？

男 1：Windows 98。我想它有點過時了。

男 2：有點？你真是隻恐龍耶。你的軟體該升級了。

男 1：要怎麼做？

男 2：我教你。你的文件都有備份嗎？

男 1：呃……

男 2：真是令人難以置信。把電腦開機，然後把你的資料存在 USB 隨身碟裡。你最好把你的通訊錄也複製起來比較好。

男 1：我的什麼？

男 2：你是昨天才出生的啊？把圖示拖放到這兒。

男 1：什麼是圖示？

男 2：我甚至不想回答這問題。現在把這片光碟放進去。按這裡就可安裝軟體，然後再重新啟動電腦。

男 1：我的電腦穿了靴子？

男 2：別耍寶了。天啊，已經沒有剩餘空間了。你這裡面存了些什麼檔案？

男 1：什麼都有。自從我拿到這台電腦後，就從來沒刪過東西。

男 2：把這些舊東西都刪了，電子郵件也都清空。

男 1：哎喲！我把茶灑到鍵盤上了。

男 2：真不知道你是怎麼存活在這辦公室裡……或者我該說，是怎麼存活在 21 世紀的！

【單字片語】

❶ make ~ crazy：令～抓狂
❷ turn ~ off：關閉～
❸ out of date：過時
❹ dinosaur：恐龍（指跟不上時代的人）
❺ I'll show you.：我教你。
❻ document：文件
❼ be born yesterday：昨天出生（指人無知）
❽ clear out ~：清空
❾ survive：生存；殘存

Quick Check

讓我們一起來複習本章所介紹過的句型！請依據以下中文句子的意思，來完成對應的英文句子。（答案就在本頁最下方。）

❶ 我把手機設成靜音模式。→P122

I ( ) my cellphone to ( ) ( ).

❷ 我將電腦初始化。→P125

I ( ) the computer.

❸ 我把電子郵件轉寄給相關人員。→P127

I ( ) the e-mail to the people ( ).

❹ 我用搜尋引擎尋找一些網站。→P128

I ( ) ( ) some websites with the ( ) ( ).

❺ 我的手機現在沒訊號，因為我在地下室。→P130

My cellphone ( ) ( ) ( ) ( ) now because
( ) ( ) ( ) ( ).

❻ 我沒有使用無限上網方案，卻看了好多影片。→P132

I ( ) a lot of videos ( ) ( ) the ( )
( ) ( ).

❼ 這和 Mac 不相容，對吧？→P132

That's not ( ), ( ) ( )?

❽ 這電腦讓我很洩氣，因為它開機實在很慢。→P134

The computer ( ) me ( ) because it ( ) so long
to ( ).

❾ 在網路上申請比較便宜。→P136

It's cheaper ( ) you ( ) ( ).

❿ 我一個禮拜沒用電腦，所以要回覆這期間累積的所有電子郵件是很艱鉅的任務。
→P140

I didn't ( ) my computer for a week, so it's going to be a ( )
( ) to ( ) all the e-mails that ( ) ( ) ( ).

---

❶ set/silent/mode ❷ initialize ❸ forward/
concerned ❹ look/for/search/engine ❺
is/out/of/service/I'm/in/the/basement ❻
watched/without/using/unlimited/download/

package ❼ Mac-compatible/is/it ❽ makes/
frustrated/takes/boot ❾ if/apply/online ❿
use/big/job/answer/piled/up/meanwhile

chapter 6 Relaxing at Home

在家放鬆

假日終於能在家舒緩放鬆。
本章提供如看電視、打電動、
穿著睡衣發呆等等消磨時間的方法。
一起學習「悠閒懶散」相關的動作
及內心想法之表達吧！

Words 單字篇

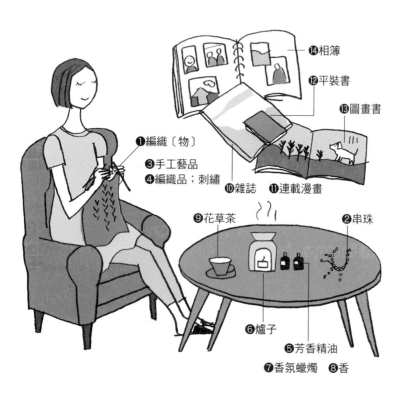

⑭相簿

⑫平裝書

⑬圖畫書

①編織〔物〕

③手工藝品
④編織品；刺繡

⑩雜誌　⑪連載漫畫

⑨花草茶

②串珠

⑥爐子

⑤芳香精油

⑦香氛蠟燭　⑧香

❶ knitting　❷ beadwork　❸ handicraft　❹ fancywork　❺ aroma oil
❻ burner　❼ scented candle　❽ incense　❾ herbal tea　❿ magazine
⓫ comic series　⓬ paperback　⓭ picture book　⓮ photo album

首先，讓我們透過各種物品的名稱，
來掌握「在家放鬆」給人的整體印象。

❶有線電視
❶衛星播送
❶數位播送
❷卡通
❷八卦節目
❷連續劇

❶電視
❶頻道

❷撲克牌
❷棋盤遊戲
❷電動
❷遙控器

❶ television　❶ channel　❶ cable television　❶ satellite broadcasting
❶ digital broadcasting　❷ cartoon　❷ gossip show　❷ drama series
❷ video game　❷ remote control　❷ board game　❷ cards

1 我換台。
I change the channel.

2 我不斷地切換電視頻道。
I surf the TV channels.

3 我把電視節目錄在硬碟機裡。
I record a show on a hard-disk recorder.

4 我一個人看綜藝節目。
I watch a variety show alone.

5 我和家人一起打電動。
I play a video game with my family.

tips

❷ channel <u>surfing</u>/<u>zapping</u> 就是「不停切換頻道」之意。而「遙控器」說成 remote control。

❹ alone是「獨自地」，為副詞。alone亦可作形容詞用，例如 He is alone in the house.（他獨自一個人在家）。

❺「電動」也可說成 computer game，而「沉迷於電動」可說成 be hooked on video games。

6 我在網上預訂票券。
I pre-order a ticket online.

7 我把新歌下載到我的 iPod 裡。
I download new songs to my iPod.

8 我編織東西。
I do some knitting (fancywork).

9 我做串珠。
I do some beadwork.

10 我做些園藝工作。
I do the gardening.

❻ online 是指「在網路上」，而「預售票」則說成 advance ticket。
❼「在網路上購買音樂」可說成 purchase music on the Internet。
❽「製作手工藝品」可說成 make handicrafts。另外「最愛的消遣娛樂」則是 favorite pastime。
❾「用串珠做手工藝品」就是 make things with beads。

11 我和朋友講很久的電話。
I have a long phone chat with my friend.

12 我整理相簿。
I sort out photo albums.

13 我點香並放鬆。
I burn incense and relax.

14 我一邊翻閱我最愛的雜誌,一邊喝花草茶。
I flip through my favorite magazine while drinking herbal tea.

15 我一整天啥事兒都沒做。
I spend the day doing nothing.

tips

⓫ chat 就是「聊天」,而「和朋友講很久的電話」也可說成 talk with one's friend for a long time on the phone。

⓬ 「把照片收集起來放進相簿」可說成 put pictures together for a photo album,而「沖印照片」則叫 print a photo。

⓭ 「芳香療法」說成 aromatherapy,「點香氛蠟燭」則說成 burn scented candles。aroma 和 scent 都指「香氣」。

16 我整天都穿著睡衣。

I stay in my pajamas all day.

17 我補眠。

I catch up on my sleep.

18 我打開一罐啤酒。

I open a can of beer.

19 我叫外送比薩。

I order a delivery pizza.

20 我沒化妝就到附近的便利商店去。

I go to the nearby convenience store without putting any makeup on.

⑭ 「泡花草茶」就說成 make herbal tea。

⑮ 「打發時間」說成 pass the time。

⑰ catch up on ~ 是指「彌補〔不足的部分〕」。而「午睡」可說成 take a nap。

⑲ 「宅配」叫 home-delivery service，而「叫外送」則說成 order out。

1　現在的電視頻道實在多得不知從何選起。
Nowadays, there are too many TV channels to choose from.

2　這個時段沒有任何好節目。
There aren't any good programs at this hour.

3　我在搶看我最愛的電視頻道時搶輸了。
I lost a fight over my favorite channel.

4　最近的外國影集都拍得很好。
Recent foreign dramas are really well-made.

5　這部電影我每看必哭。
This movie makes me cry every time I watch it.

6　這位演員真的很獨特。
This actor is really unique.

nowadays = 如今；現在╱choose from ~ = 從~中選擇

此例句也可說成 It's difficult to select a TV program because there are too many channels.。另外「數位電視」可說成 digital broadcasting，「衛星電視」則為 satellite broadcasting。另，「有線電視」是 cable <u>TV</u> / <u>television</u>，而「電視台」則叫 TV station。

---

at this hour = 在這個時段

「好節目」也指 interesting programs（有趣的節目）或 a program worth watching（值得看的節目）。至於「愚蠢（無聊）的節目」就說成 silly (boring) programs。

---

lose a fight over ~ = 在搶~時輸了 *cf.* lost < lose

「看某人最喜歡的電視節目」說成 watch one's favorite TV <u>show</u>/<u>program</u>。

---

foreign drama = 外國影集 *cf.* <u>TV</u> / <u>television</u> drama = 電視劇╱well-made = 製作精良 *cf.* poorly-made = 製作品質不好

與電視劇相關的詞彙還有 script（腳本；劇本）、starring ~（~主演）等。

---

movie (= film) = 電影 *cf.* cinema = 電影（集合詞）╱make ~ cry = 使~哭泣 *cf.* make ~ laugh = 讓~發笑

「盡情哭泣」說成 have a good cry，而「哭完後感覺很痛快」可說成 feel great after crying。

---

actor = 演員 *cf.* actress = 女演員╱leading actor = 男主角╱supporting actor = 男配角╱role = 角色

這裡除了用 unique（獨特的）之外，也可用 impressive（令人印象深刻的）、appealing（有魅力的）等形容詞。

7　我們最近都沒看到那個藝人了。
We don't see that TV personality anymore these days.

8　我忙得沒空看錄下來的電視節目。要全部看完得花不少時間。
I'm too busy to watch recorded TV programs. It takes a lot of time to watch them all.

9　現在我要看我錄的〔連續劇〕最後一集了！
Now, I'm going to watch the final episode [of the drama series] that I recorded!

10　哇！他們竟然已經開始重播那部戲了。
Wow. They are already rebroadcasting that drama.

11　我看有英文字幕而且是以英語發音的 DVD 時，可以學到很多。
I can learn a lot when I watch a DVD in English with English subtitles.

12　這些 DVD 逾期了！我租了 3 支但是卻沒能全部看完。
These DVDs are overdue! I rented three but couldn't watch them all.

TV personality = 電視人物；出現在電視上的藝人 cf. celebrity = 名人；名流
personality 亦可指一個人的「個性」或「性格」。

---

too busy to ～ = 太忙以至於無法做～／recorded = 錄下來的／it takes time to
～ = 做～要花時間
此例句也可改為 I don't have enough time to watch all those recorded TV
programs. 。

---

final episode = 最後一集／drama series = 連續劇
episode 指電視劇或影集的「一集」。而一般連續劇通常會從「前情提要」
Previously on ... 開始，最後則以「待續」To be continued. 作結。

---

rebroadcast = 重播～ cf. broadcast = 播出～／rerun (= repeat) = 重播
此例句也可說成 Wow! They are already repeating this drama. 。而「這個節
目是重播的」可說成 This program is a rerun. 。

---

learn a lot = 學到很多／watch a DVD in English = 看以英語發音的DVD／
subtitle (= caption) = 字幕
此例句中的 I can learn a lot ... 也可改成 It's a good way to learn ... （……是
很好的學習方法）。

---

overdue = 過期的；逾期的 cf. due = 到期的／rent = 租借～ cf. rental = 租賃的；
出租的／borrow = 借來／lend = 借給／return = 歸還
「歸還日」說成 <u>due</u> / <u>return</u> date。

13 我今天想聽比利喬的歌。
I feel like listening to Billy Joel today.

14 這首歌令人覺得很舒緩。
This song is really soothing.

15 每次都要換 CD 好麻煩。
It's a bother to switch CDs each time.

16 我打電動打到深夜，所以今天早上有黑眼圈。
I was playing a video game till late at night, so I have dark circles under my eyes this morning.

17 我等不及要看這部連載漫畫的下一集。
I can hardly wait to read the next story in this comic series.

18 我有好幾本書都只看了一半。
I have several half-finished books.

feel like ~ = 覺得想要~／listen to ~ = 傾聽~；聆聽~

「我沒有聽~的心情」可說成 I'm in no mood to listen to ~。另，「熱門歌曲」叫 hit [song]；「跟著一起唱」是 sing along；「哼歌」是 hum。「用 iPod 播放歌曲」則是 play music on an iPod。

---

soothing = 使人平靜、放鬆的 e.g. soothing music = 舒緩心情的音樂

此例句也可改成 I feel comforted when I listen to this song.。

It's a bother to ~ = 做~很麻煩／switch = 轉換~／each time = 每次

由於是要「替換」，所以 CDs 要用複數。「把 CD 放進播放器」可說成 put a CD in [to] the CD player，而「播放 CD」則是 play a CD。

---

video game = 電動／dark circles under one's eyes = 黑眼圈 cf. puffy eyes = 浮腫的雙眼；眼袋

「沉迷於電動」可說成 be into / hooked on video games，而「上網打電動」是 play a game online。至於「遊樂場」則叫 video / game arcade。

---

can hardly ~ = 幾乎無法~／comic = 漫畫 cf. cartoon = 卡通／comic book = 漫畫書／comic strip =〔報紙等的〕連環漫畫／comic series = 連載漫畫

源自日本的「漫畫」現在在英語中也可直接使用日文的 manga 來表達。

---

several = 幾個／half-finished = 進行到一半還沒完成的；半成品的 cf. finished = 完成的／half-read book = 讀到一半的書

「一口氣讀完」可說成 read a book in / at one sitting。「從頭讀到尾」則是 read a book from cover to cover。

19 我們何不一起來玩 UNO 或什麼其他遊戲？
Why don't we play Uno or something together?

20 我的收集還差一點就要完成了！
Just a bit more and my collection is almost completed!

21 我就是為這口啤酒而活的。
I'm living for this gulp of beer.

22 我這才想起來，我有一瓶別人送的葡萄酒。
Now I remember I have a bottle of wine I was given as a gift.

23 有包裹快遞？！怎麼辦？我這身打扮是不能應門的。
A parcel delivery?! What do I do? I can't answer the door in this outfit.

24 我剛起床，所以我要假裝不在家。
I just got up, so I'll pretend I'm not home.

Why don't we ~? = 我們何不~？／play = 玩〔遊戲〕e.g. play chess (cards) = 下棋（玩牌）／~ or something = ~或什麼的

「使用牌卡的遊戲」叫 card game，而「使用棋盤的遊戲」則叫 board game。

---

just a bit more = 只要再多一點／collection = 收集〔品〕；收藏〔品〕／complete = 完成

a bit（一點點）可用 a little 來替換。「收集~」說成 collect ~ 或 make a collection of ~。「CD（硬幣／古董／藝術品）的收藏」就叫 CD (coin/antique/art) collection。

---

live for ~ = 為了~而活 e.g. have something (nothing) to live for = 人生活得有（沒）意義／gulp = 一大口 e.g. finish the drink at one gulp = 把酒一口喝光

「酒鬼」叫 alcoholic/drunk/drunkard。

---

remember = 想到~／a bottle of ~ = 一瓶~／given as a gift = 一件別人送的禮物

歐美國家習慣在去朋友家吃飯時帶瓶酒或是甜點，用意類似我們的伴手禮。客人有時候也會事先直接詢問主人 Could I bring something? Some wine? A cake?

---

parcel delivery = 包裹快遞／parcel (= package) = 包裹／answer the door = 應門／in ~ outfit = 以~的打扮／outfit = 整套服裝 e.g. How do you like my outfit? = 你覺得我這副打扮如何？

「用快遞送包裹」可說成 send a parcel/package by delivery service，而「收件」則是 receive the parcel/package。

I just got up = 我剛剛才起床／pretend = 假裝／not home = 不在家 e.g. My husband is not home. = 我先生不在家

也可用 I'll pretend to be out.（我會假裝已出門了）這種說法。

Skit 🏠 在家放鬆篇

假日情侶在家度過悠閒時光

Woman: **What should we do about dinner tonight? I don't feel like❶ cooking.**

Man: **I'll order delivery pizza. And we can open a couple of cans of beer.**

W: **Now I remember I have a bottle of wine I was given as a gift. Let's open that, too!**

M: **After dinner, do you want to watch On Golden Pond? I recorded it on the DVD recorder.**

W: **Oh, that movie makes me cry every time I watch it.**

M: **OK. I know what!❷ Some of the recent American dramas are really well-made. We can find one of those on TV.**

W: **There aren't any programs worth watching at this hour.**

M: **We could play a game instead❸. Why don't we play chess or something together?**

W: **That sounds good❹. I'll put on some music❺. I feel like listening to Billy Joel today.**

M: **I love his music. Play his new album. Those songs are really soothing.**

W: **Oh! A parcel delivery? What do I do? I can't go to the door in this outfit.**

M: **What are you talking about? You look fine.**

W: **Are you crazy? My shirt is dirty and my hair is a mess❻!**

M: **Don't worry. I'll get the door. You order the pizza. And brush your hair.**

W: **Ha, ha, ha. You're such a funny guy.**

女子：今天的晚飯該怎麼辦？我並不想做飯。

男子：我會叫外送比薩。我們還可以開幾罐啤酒來喝。

女：我這才想起來，我有一瓶別人送的葡萄酒。咱們也開來喝吧！

男：晚飯後，想不想看電影《金色池塘》？我錄在 DVD 錄影機裡了。

女：喔，那部電影我每看必哭。

男：好吧。我有好主意！最近有些美國影集拍得很不錯。我們可以在電視
　　上選一部來看。

女：這時段沒什麼值得看的節目。

男：那我們改玩遊戲吧。我們何不一起下棋或玩點什麼其他的？

女：聽起來不錯。我來放一些音樂。我今天想聽比利喬的歌。

男：我很喜歡他的音樂。放他的新專輯吧。那些歌令人覺得很舒緩。

女：啊！有包裹快遞？怎麼辦？我這身打扮是不能應門的。

男：妳在說什麼啊？妳看起來很好啊。

女：你瘋了嗎？我的襯衫這麼髒，頭髮又一團亂！

男：別擔心。我來應門。妳去叫比薩，順便梳個頭。

女：哈，哈，哈。你真是個有趣的傢伙。

【單字片語】

❶ feel like -ing：覺得想做～

❷ I know what：我有好主意。

❸ instead：代替

❹ sounds good：聽起來不錯

❺ put on music：放音樂

❻ mess：一團亂

Quick Check

讓我們一起來複習本章所介紹過的句型！請依據以下中文句子的意思，來完成對應的英文句子。（答案就在本頁最下方。）

❶ 我點香並放鬆。 →P154

I ( ) ( ) and relax.

❷ 我補眠。 →P155

I ( ) ( ) ( ) my sleep.

❸ 我在搶看我最愛的電視頻道時搶輸了。 →P156

I ( ) ( ) ( ) ( ) my favorite stations.

❹ 我看有英文字幕而且是以英語發音的 DVD 時，可以學到很多。 →P158

I ( ) ( ) ( ) ( ) when I watch a DVD
( ) ( ) with English ( ).

❺ 這些 DVD 逾期了！我租了 3 支但是卻沒能全部看完。 →P158

These DVDs are ( )! I ( ) three but ( )
( ) ( ) ( ).

❻ 每次都要換 CD 好麻煩。 →P160

( ) a ( ) ( ) switch CDs ( ) ( ).

❼ 我等不及要看這連載漫畫的下一集。 →P160

I ( ) ( ) ( ) ( ) read the next story
( ) this comic series.

❽ 我有好幾本書都只看了一半。 →P160

I have ( ) ( ) books.

❾ 我就是為這口啤酒而活的。 →P162

( ) ( ) ( ) this ( ) ( ) beer.

❿ 我剛起床，所以我要假裝不在家。 →P162

I ( ) ( ) ( ), so I'll ( ) I'm ( )
( ).

---

❶ burn/incense ❷ catch/up/on ❸ lost/ a/fight/over ❹ can/learn/a/lot/in/English/ subtitles ❺ overdue/rented/couldn't/watch/ them/all ❻ It's/bother/to/each/time ❼ can/ hardly/wait/to/in ❽ several/half-finished ❾ I'm/living/for/gulp/of ❿ just/got/up/pretend/ not/home

chapter 7 Going Out on a Day Off

假日外出

假日與朋友或情人相約出門，
不論是約會、購物、看電影或開車兜風，
本章收錄了可用於各種出遊情境的例句，
而這些動作的敘述及想法的表達
也都可應用於會話中喔！

Words 單字篇

⑪景點
⑩摩天輪
⑧鬼屋
⑦遊樂園
⑨雲霄飛車
②會面地點 ③咖啡廳 ①等待的時間
⑥數位相機
⑤約會
④盛裝

❶ wait time ❷ meeting place ❸ coffee shop ❹ Sunday best
❺ date ❻ digital camera ❼ amusement park ❽ haunted house
❾ roller coaster ❿ Ferris wheel ⓫ attraction ⓬ theater

首先，讓我們透過各種物品的名稱，
來掌握「假日外出」給人的整體印象。

⑮預告片
⑯上映
⑰限制級電影

⑫電影院
⑬電影

⑱招待券

⑭保留位

㉓試衣間

㉒店員；銷售員

㉔特賣
㉕特價商品

㉑價格標籤

⑲購物中心　⑳商店

⑬ movie ⑭ reserved seat ⑮ trailer ⑯ showing ⑰ R-rated movie
⑱ complimentary ticket ⑲ shopping center ⑳ shop ㉑ price tag
㉒ sales clerk ㉓ fitting room ㉔ sale ㉕ bargain

1 我和我男朋友在咖啡廳見面。
I meet my boyfriend at a coffee shop.

2 我把會面地點用電子郵件寄給他。
I e-mail him about the meeting place.

3 我選出我最棒的服裝。
I pick out my Sunday best.

4 他臨時取消了我們的約會。
He canceled our date at the last minute.

5 我們夜間出遊。
We have a night out.

tips

❸ Sunday best 一詞源於「週日去教會做禮拜時穿的最體面服裝」。
❹「放～鴿子」英文用 stand ~ up。
❺「一整晚」是 all night，例如 I drink all night.。
❻ hang out 是「閒混」的意思。mall 指「購物商場（中心）」

6 我們在購物商場閒晃。
We hang out at the mall.

7 我把男友（女友）介紹給家人認識。
I introduce my boyfriend (girlfriend) to my family.

8 我和一個女孩搭訕。（我被一個傢伙搭訕。）
I hit on a girl. (I was hit on by a guy.)

9 我和朋友嘰哩呱啦連續聊好幾個小時。
I chatter away with friends for hours on end.

10 我們在一個朋友家開火鍋派對。
We have a hotpot party at a friend's place.

❽ hit on～指「與～搭訕」。
❾ chatter 指「喋喋不休地談論不關痛癢的事」。一般的「閒聊」則可用 chat 表達。

11 我去購物。
I go shopping.

12 我到幾家百貨公司購物。
I shop around at some department stores.

13 我試穿衣物。
I try something on.

14 我在書店站著看書。
I stand and read in a bookstore.

15 我在園藝中心買了些園藝用品。
I pick up some gardening supplies at a garden center.

tips

⓬ window-shopping 指「瀏覽商店櫥窗（而不購物）」。
⓮ 「〔在書店中〕瀏覽書籍」可用 browse 表達。
⓯ 專賣園藝用品的地方就叫 garden center，而「擅長園藝」則說成 have a green thumb。

16 我開車兜風。
I go for a drive.

17 我在收費亭付費。
I pay at the toll booth.

18 我使用 ETC系統。
I use the ETC(Electronic Toll Collection) system.

19 我的車壞了，於是打電話找拖吊車。
My car breaks down and I call a tow truck.

20 我被假日返鄉車潮給困住了。
I get stuck in returning holiday traffic.

⓲ 在會話中，有時會用 spin（兜一圈）這個字來表示兜風，例如 go for a spin in a car。
⓱ toll 就是「通行費」。
⓴「塞車」是 traffic jam。

21 我去看電影（戲劇／音樂劇）。
I go to see a movie (play/musical).

22 我上舞蹈課。
I take dancing lessons.

23 我參加一群同好的聚會。
I attend a gathering of people with the same hobby.

24 我拼命運動，流了一身汗。
I play sports very hard, and work up a good sweat.

25 我在棒球打擊練習場紓解壓力。
I relieve stress at the batting center.

tips

㉒ take lessons 就是「上課」的意思。
㉔ work up ~ 有「激發（食慾或興趣等）」的意思。
㉕「感到壓力很大」說成 get stressed out，而「應付壓力」則
　說成 cope with stress。
㉖ cheer for ~ 是「替～加油」。

26 我替我最愛的社區棒球隊加油。
I cheer for my favorite neighborhood baseball team.

27 我們在河畔烤肉。
We have a barbecue at the riverside.

28 我去探索一個陌生的城鎮。
I explore an unfamiliar town.

29 我在跳蚤市場賣東西。
I sell stuff at a flea market.

30 我做義工。
I do volunteer work.

㉙ flea 就是「跳蚤」，而此語之起源眾說紛紜，有人說是因為一開始在 market 賣的東西上有跳蚤，也有人說是因為群聚的人們從遠處看來就像跳蚤一般。

㉚ 「參加義工活動」就說成 I take part in volunteer work.。

1　你確定是約在這裡嗎？
Are you sure this is the meeting place?

2　我的手機有留言。
I've got a message on my cell.

3　很抱歉我會晚到，但是我就快到了。你可以再等 5 分鐘嗎？
Sorry I'm _running/going to be_ late but I'm almost there. Can you wait another five minutes?

4　我知道你有手機，但也別每一次都遲到。
I know you have a cellphone, but don't be late every single time.

5　我好久沒約會了。該穿什麼去呢？
It's been a while since I had a date. What should I wear?

6　你今天看來真時髦！
You look pretty sharp today!

meeting place = 會面地點

Are you sure ~?（你確定～嗎？）也可説成 You sure ~?。在較不正式的對話中，有時就會省略 be 動詞，例如 You ready to go?（你準備好要出發了嗎？）。

've got (=have got) = 有／cell (=cellphone) =手機

欲表達「在〔機器等東西的〕裡面」時，介系詞不用 in，而要用 on，例如 I have some important documents on my USB drive.（我的 USB 隨身碟裡存了些重要文件）。

---

be running late = 比預定的〔進度〕慢／almost = 幾乎／another ~ = 再～

I'm almost there. 就是「我快到了」的意思。而「抱歉，我遲到了」就説成 Sorry, I'm late.。

---

cellphone (= <u>cellular phone</u> / <u>mobile phone</u>) = 手機／every single time = 每一次

every single ~ 是「每一個」之意。every day 是「每天」，而若用 every single day 的話，就有強調「每一天」的意思。

---

have a date = 去約會

It's been a while since ~ 就是「自從～以來，有好一陣子了」。「好久不見」可用 It's been a while. 來表達。

---

look ~ = 看起來～／sharp =〔外觀打扮〕時髦的；漂亮的

sharp 這個形容詞除了「尖鋭的」外，還有其他很多意義，例如 be sharp at ~（在～方面很敏鋭；擅長～）、sharp taste（強烈的味道）、sharp walk（輕快的腳步）等。

7　我們何不先喝點茶，並計畫一下今天的行程？
Why don't we have some tea first and make plans for the rest of the day?

8　你不覺得這樣偶爾把小孩交給褓母，然後咱們夫妻倆單獨約個會很不錯嗎？
Don't you think this is good — leaving our kids with a babysitter and spending time alone together once in a while?

9　你知道嗎？美術館現在正在舉辦畢卡索的展覽。
You know what? The museum is holding a Picasso exhibition now.

10　咱們去漫畫咖啡廳消磨時間吧。
Let's hang out in a manga café.

11　我們的約會總是一成不變，不過只要能和他在一起我就很開心。
Our dating is stuck in a rut. I'm happy just to be with him, though.

12　天氣這麼好，出去走走如何？
How about doing something outside because it's such a beautiful day?

make plans for ~ = 為～做計畫／the rest of ~ = ～的剩餘部分

Why don't we ~? 就是「我們何不～？」之意，常用於提議時，比 Let's ~（讓我們做～）客氣，但又比 Shall we ~?（我們是否該～？）隨興。

---

leave A with B = 把 A 交給 B／alone together = 僅兩人一起相處／once in a while = 偶爾

Don't you think ~? 為否定問句，表示「你不覺得～嗎？」。需注意的是，若要回答「我也這麼認為」，就說成 Yes, I do.，而「我不覺得」則應說成 No, I don't.。

---

hold = 舉辦～／exhibition = 展覽

You know what? 就是「你知道嗎？」的意思，用於切入話題時。類似的表達方式還有 Guess what?（你猜怎麼樣？）。

---

hang out = 閒晃；消磨時間／manga café = 漫畫咖啡廳

hang out 就是「悠閒地打發時間」之意，而 idle away 也有「悠閒地打發～」之意。如 I often idle away my holiday watching TV.（我經常看電視打發週末時光）。

---

be stuck in a rut = 一成不變的／rut = 車輪形成的凹痕；常規／though = 不過（副詞，常置於句尾）

「脫離慣例；追求變化」可說成 get out of a rut。另外，「變得一成不變」則是 become routine，例如 My life's become routine.（我的生活變得一成不變）。

How about -ing? = 去做～如何？（向對方提議、表達建議之說法）／outside = 在外面；在戶外

本句中 a beautiful day 可用 a nice day 來代替。而 a fine day 是「晴天」之意，但不見得是 a beautiful day。

13 電影院現在有好片子可看嗎？
Is there a good movie at the theater now?

14 我有多餘的招待券。你願意跟我一起去嗎？
I have an extra complimentary ticket. Would you like to go with me?

15 這部片昨天下檔！真掃興！
The movie ended yesterday! What a bummer!

16 在下一場開演前，我們還有很多時間。
We have plenty of time until the next show.

17 你覺得換一部片子看如何？這部今天太多人看了。
What do you say to trying another movie? This one's too crowded today.

18 我們對電影的品味相當不同。
We have quite different tastes in movies.

theater = 電影院（英國偏好用 cinema）

「正在播～；～正在上映」要用不及物動詞 show，例如 *Departures* is showing at the theater now.（*Departures* 現在正在電影院上映）。

---

extra = 多餘的／complimentary = 免費的；贈送的

「〔免費〕招待券」也可說成 invitation ticket 或 comp（complimentary 的簡稱）。而 Would you like to ~? 是用於邀約對方時的句型，在此也可說成 What do you say to going with me?。

---

end = 結束／bummer = 令人失望的事

類似 What a bummer! 的說法還有 I'm very disappointed.（我很失望），或是 How unlucky!（真衰！）。

---

plenty of ~ = 很多的～；充足的～／show = 演出；播映

此例句若改為否定，就說 We don't have much time before the next show.

What do you say to -ing? = 你覺得做～如何？／crowded = 人多擁擠的

What do you say to -ing? 直譯成中文就是「對於～，你會說什麼？」而這其實是表示「做～如何？」之意。

---

quite different = 相當不同／taste = 品味；喜好的類型

taste 這個單字經常用來表達「品味」之意，例如 She has good taste in clothes.（她對衣服很有品味）。另外，There is no accounting for taste. 是指「青菜蘿蔔各有所好」。這句話的原意是「品味是無法解釋、沒有理由的」。

19 你不跟我一起去購物嗎？今天有特價喔。

Won't you come shopping with me? There's a sale today.

20 我不介意陪她一起購物，但是每次都要花好多時間。

I don't mind going shopping with her, but it always takes so much time.

21 我一直很想來這家店。

I've always wanted to come to this shop.

22 哇！這隊伍排得真長。才開店 10 分鐘耶。

Wow! That sure is a long line. It only opened 10 minutes ago.

23 特賣是值得等待的。

It was worth waiting for the sale.

24 既然我們來了，就不能錯過 A 店和 B 店，對吧？

Since we're here, we can't miss going to Shop A and Shop B, can we?

sale = 出售；特價拍賣 cf. bargain = 特價品

Won't you ~? 是用來表達「做～如何？」（提議）或「可以為我做～嗎？」（請託）等意思的疑問句型，比 Will you ~?客氣。而若像 Won't you please ~? 這樣再加上 please，就能再進一步增加禮貌程度。

---

don't mind -ing = 不介意做～ cf. mind = 介意～／go -ing = 去做～／take time = 花時間

「你介意做～嗎？」就說成 Would you mind -ing?。若是「介意，不想做」就回答 Yes, I would.，而若是「不介意，願意做」，則可說 No, I wouldn't.。

---

have always wanted to ~ = 一直都很想做～

always 這個字一般給人的印象都是與現在式一同使用時的「總是」之意，但若用於現在完成式或未來式中，便有「一直不變地～」的意思，例如 I will always love you.（我會一直愛你）。

Wow! = 哇（表示驚訝的感嘆詞）／line = 隊伍；行列

代表「確實；的確」之意的副詞 sure 通常放在主詞與 be 動詞之間（如本句），和形容詞的 sure（確信的；有把握的）用法不同，例如 The man is sure of his success.（此人深信自己會成功）。另，此例句的後半句也可說成 It's only been 10 minutes since it opened.。

---

be worth -ing = 值得做～

worth 這個形容詞很特殊，它後面可接動名詞（如本句）或名詞，例如 It's worth a try.（這值得一試）。另，此例句也可改以 The sale 為主詞，說成 The sale is worth waiting for.。

---

since ~ = 既然～；因為～／miss -ing = 錯過～；漏掉～

miss 在這裡是「錯過～」之意。為人指引路線時，最後常常會加上 You can't miss it.（你絕不可能錯過它 = 一定會看到它）這種固定的說法。

25 我很好奇這間店今天怎麼這麼空。
I wonder why this shop isn't busy today.

26 拒絕店員的推薦對我而言很困難。
It's difficult for me to turn down what a sales clerk recommends.

27 嗯……牛仔褲的價格範圍很廣。
Hmm ... the price of jeans runs the gamut.

28 我打算買這個！
I'm going to buy this!

29 超過我的預算了……怎麼辦呢？。
That's over my budget ... what <u>shall</u>/<u>should</u> I do?

30 我要用我的獎金來買！
I'll pay for it with my bonus!

I wonder why ~ = 我很好奇為何～；我在想為何～

wonder 之後接著用 if 或疑問詞（what、why、how 等）所引導的名詞子句，例如 I wonder what I should buy for my girlfriend.（我在想該買給我女友什麼好）。

---

turn down ~ = 拒絕～／sales clerk = 店員／recommend = 推薦

「我不擅長應付店員」可以説 I'm not good at dealing with sales clerks. 或 I'm not comfortable with sales clerks.。

---

run the gamut = 範圍很廣／run = 涵蓋〔範圍〕／gamut = 整個範圍；全音域

「〔商店的〕商品種類齊全（很少）」可用 wide (narrow) selection，例如 The bookstore offers a wide selection of books for children.（該書店的童書種類非常齊全）。

---

be going to ~ = 打算～

will 或 be going to~ 都能用來表達未來的預定動作，但是以本例這種狀況來説，若用 will，説成 I will buy this! 的話，就會變成「無論怎樣我都要買這個！」這樣強烈的態度（請參考第 30 個例句）。

---

budget = 預算

「〔預算〕吃緊」就用 tight 來表達，例如 I'm on a tight budget so I can't afford this.（我的預算吃緊，所以買不起這個）。

---

with = 用／bonus = 獎金

「一次付清」可説成 pay a lump-sum / something off in full；「分期付款」則是 pay on time / in installments（installment 是指分期付款中的一期），如 I'd like to pay in installments.（我想分期付款）。

31 我在一家百貨公司地下室的食品區試吃，結果竟然覺得飽了。
I end up feeling full trying out the food samples on the basement food floor of a department store.

32 所有的停車場都滿了。
All the parking lots are full.

33 哇，這隧道真長！
Wow, isn't this tunnel long!

34 前方塞車塞了 10 公里。
Traffic's backed up for 10 kilometers ahead.

35 我很驚訝我的新車竟然如此省油。
I'm amazed how fuel-efficient my new car is.

36 從現在起是環保駕駛的時代了。
Eco-driving is here to stay.

end up [-ing] = 結果變成～〔狀態〕／feel full = 感覺飽了／try out ～ = 試用～；試吃～／sample = 樣品／basement = 地下室

「美食街」、「美食廣場」可以說成 food court。

parking lot = 停車場 cf. parking garage = 室內停車場／metered parking space = 按錶收費的停車場

「停車場」在英國一般稱為 car park。注意，park 可做為動詞使用，意思就是「停車」，例如 There's no space to park our car.（我們的車沒地方可停）。

tunnel = 隧道

由於本句用了 isn't ～，故乍看之下像是個疑問句，但是這其實是表示「真是很～！」的驚嘆句型。

be backed up = 因塞車而車流回堵／ahead = 前方

與「塞車」相關的表達方式還有：We're stuck in bumper-to-bumper gridlock.（我們被困在動彈不得的車陣中）、Traffic is inching/crawling along.（車流緩慢移動）、We should set off early to beat the traffic jams.（我們應該早點出發以避開塞車）等。

amazed = 驚訝的／be fuel-efficient (= get good mileage) = 省油；燃油效率高的

在會話中可用動詞 rock 來表達「真棒；很讚」之意，例如 Wow, this car rocks!（哇，這車有夠讚！）。而相反的「很爛；真糟」則用動詞 suck，例如 This car sucks! It gets terrible mileage.（這車真爛！太耗油了）。

eco-driving = 環保駕駛／～be here to stay = 從現在起是～的時代

be here to stay 原意是「〔新事物或觀念〕在此固定下來」，也就指「從現在起是～的時代了」。而若想針對人表達「從現在起是他的時代了」這類的意思時，則要說成 His time has come.。

37 我希望能和男友一起欣賞這樣浪漫的景色。

I hope I can see a romantic view like that with my boyfriend.

38 那遊樂園很好玩。我可是能在那兒待上好幾個小時的。

The amusement park's fun. I could spend hours there.

39 到處都是星巴克、優衣庫、麥當勞……現在每個城鎮都失去了獨特性。

Starbucks, Uniqlo, McDonald's ... Every town is losing its individuality these days.

40 我已經走不動了。

My legs feel like lead already.

41 假如是平日這裡人少的時候，我們就會覺得更輕鬆一些。

We'd feel more relaxed if it was a weekday with fewer people here.

42 嘿，竟然已經這麼晚了。

Hey, look at the time.

romantic = 浪漫的；羅曼蒂克的／view = 景色；風景

用 I hope I can ~ 表示是可能性較高的希望；若是用 I wish I could ~ 則表示不可能的希望，例如 I wish I could fly.（我希望我能夠飛）。

---

amusement park = 遊樂園／fun = 好玩的；有趣的

本句中的 could 表達的是「如果真要的話，我是可以的」之意，並非過去式。

---

individuality = 獨特性；個別特色

lose [one's] individuality 表示「失去獨特性」，而「保留獨特性」則説成 preserve [one's] individuality。另，「強調獨特性」可以説 highlight [one's] individuality。「一個獨特的社區」則是 unique local community。

---

feel like ~ = 感覺像~／lead = 鉛（發音為 [lɛd]）

此例句直譯為中文就是「我的腳感覺就像鉛一樣」。

---

feel relaxed = 感覺輕鬆

本句表達的是「與現在事實相反」的假設。注意，動詞部分應使用過去形式：~would feel ... if it was~。（'d 為 would 的縮寫）

---

hey = 嘿（喚起對方注意的感嘆詞）／the time = 現在的時間

本句的直譯是「嘿，你看現在的時間」，而意思就是「時間不早了」。

Skit  假日外出篇

出遊計畫最終到達的目的地是⋯⋯

Man: **Hey, Shirley. Long time no see❶.**

Woman: **Yeah, sorry I haven't been around❷ lately❸. I've been really busy.**

M: **Well, we've both got the whole day off. So what do you want to do today?**

W: **How about doing something outside since it's such a beautiful day?**

M: **We could go for a drive. I'm amazed how fuel-efficient my new car is.**

W: **OK. I like to explore unfamiliar towns. Let's go see what Hikuyama is like❹.**

M: **I've been there. Starbucks, Uniqlo, McDonald's ... Every town is losing its individuality these days.**

W: **You know what? The museum is holding a Picasso exhibition now.**

M: **But today's Sunday. It'll be crowded. It'd be more relaxing if it was a weekday with fewer people.**

W: **The basement food courts of department stores are always fun. I could spend hours there.**

M: **But that will be crowded, too. Let's just hang out in a manga café.**

W: **Jeez❺. You're such a nerd❻! But I like you anyway.**

男子：嘿，雪莉，好久不見。

女子：是啊，很抱歉我最近都沒出現。我真的好忙。

男：嗯，我們兩個都休假一整天。那你今天想做些什麼呢？

女：天氣這麼好，出去走走如何？

男：我們可以開車去兜風。我的新車超省油的，讓我很驚訝呢。

女：好啊。我想去探索一下陌生的城鎮。咱們去看看低山是怎樣的地方。

男：我有去過。到處都是星巴克、優衣庫、麥當勞……現在每個城鎮都失去獨特性了。

女：你知道嗎？美術館現在正在舉辦畢卡索的展覽。

男：但是今天是週日，一定會很擠。假如是平日人少的時候去，會輕鬆得多。

女：百貨公司地下室的美食街很好玩。我可是能在那兒待上好幾個小時喔。

男：但是那裡也會很擠的。我們就在漫畫咖啡廳消磨時間就好。

女：天呀，你真是個書呆子！不過我還是很喜歡你。

【單字片語】

❶ Long time no see.：好久不見。

❷ be around：在附近

❸ lately：最近

❹ go see what ~ is like：去看看～是什麼樣子

❺ Jeez：天啊

❻ nerd：書呆子

Quick Check

讓我們一起來複習本章所介紹過的句型！請依據以下中文句子的意思，來完成對應的英文句子。（答案就在本頁最下方。）

❶ 我選出我最棒的服裝。 →P170

I ( ) ( ) my ( ) ( ).

❷ 我們在購物的商場閒晃。 →P171

We ( ) ( ) at the ( ).

❸ 我開車兜風。 →P173

I ( ) ( ) ( ) drive.

❹ 我們在河畔烤肉。 →P175

We ( ) ( ) ( ) at the riverside.

❺ 很抱歉我會晚到，但是我就快到了。你可以再等 5 分鐘嗎？ →P176

Sorry ( ) ( ) ( ) but I'm almost there. Can you wait ( ) five minutes?

❻ 這部片昨天下檔！真掃興！ →P180

The movie ( ) yesterday! ( ) ( ) ( )!

❼ 特價是值得等待的。 →P182

It was ( ) ( ) for the sale.

❽ 我很好奇這間店今天怎麼這麼空。 →P184

( ) ( ) ( ) this shop isn't ( ) today.

❾ 拒絕店員的推薦對我而言很困難。 →P184

It's ( ) ( ) ( ) to ( ) ( ) what a sales clerk recommends.

❿ 我要用我的獎金來買！ →P184

I'll ( ) ( ) it ( ) ( ) ( )!

---

❶ pick/out/Sunday/best ❷ hang/out/mall ❸ go/for/a ❹ have/a/barbecue ❺ I'm/running/late/another ❻ ended/What/a/bummer

❼ worth/waiting ❽ I/wonder/why/busy ❾ difficult/for/me/turn/down ❿ pay/for/with/my/bonus

192

chapter 8　Eating Out

外食

台灣飲食文化豐富，堪稱世界數一數二。
從高級豪華的餐廳，
到可輕鬆用餐的小吃店，
多采多姿的外食產業，
使得對味覺講究的人變得越來越多。
本章收錄了從踏進店門到結帳付款為止，
一連串動作及想法表達句型。

Words 單字篇

⓫團體聚會

❶高級餐廳

❸酒單

❷飲料

❺盤子　❹水罐

❶ classy restaurant　❷ drink　❸ wine list　❹ pitcher　❺ plate
❻ cutlery　❼ appetizer　❽ main course　❾ dessert　❿ sampler
⓫ party　⓬ tavern　⓭ food stall　⓮ shop curtain　⓯ liquor　⓰ beer

首先，讓我們透過各種物品的名稱，
來掌握「外食」給人的整體印象。

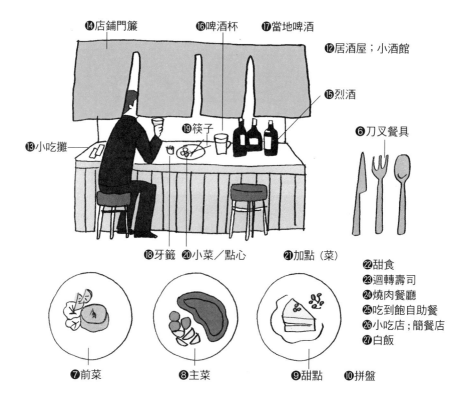

⑭店鋪門簾　⑯啤酒杯　⑰當地啤酒

⑫居酒屋；小酒館

⑮烈酒

⑲筷子

⑥刀叉餐具

⑬小吃攤

⑱牙籤　⑳小菜／點心　㉑加點（菜）

㉒甜食
㉓迴轉壽司
㉔燒肉餐廳
㉕吃到飽自助餐
㉖小吃店；簡餐店
㉗白飯

⑦前菜　　⑧主菜　　⑨甜點　⑩拼盤

mug ⑰ local beer ⑱ toothpick ⑲ chopsticks ⑳ side dish/snack
㉑ additional order ㉒ sweets ㉓ revolving sushi ㉔ *yakiniku*
restaurant ㉕ all-you-can-eat buffet ㉖ diner ㉗ steamed rice

1　我盛裝打扮去高級餐廳用餐。
I get all dressed up and go to a classy restaurant.

2　我撥開店鋪門簾走進店裡。
I enter the shop through a shop curtain.

3　我到各式各樣不同的餐廳品嚐甜食。
I try out sweets at various restaurants.

4　我告訴服務生我們的人數。
I tell the waiter how many are in our party.

5　我被要求併桌。
I am asked to share a table.

❶ get dressed up 即可表達「盛裝打扮」的意思，而若再加上 all 這個字，便可進一步強調。
❸ try out 是「嘗試～」之意，此處指「品嚐」。Various 則指「各式各樣的」。
❹「我們總共7個人」說成 We are a party of seven.。

6 我要求換座位。
I ask to change seats.

7 我請人拿菜單來。
I ask for a menu.

8 我詳讀酒單。
I peruse a wine list.

9 我問他們推薦什麼酒。
I ask what wine they recommend.

10 我確認食物是否包含任何會引起過敏的成分。
I check if the food contains any allergy-causing ingredients.

❺ 要與對方併桌時，可問 May I join you?。
❻ 「可以和你們交換座位嗎？」可說成 Would you mind switching seats?。
❿ 「對～過敏」說成 be allergic to ~，例如 I'm allergic to eggs.（我對蛋過敏）。而 ingredient 就是指「材料；成分」

11 我選（點）飲料（前菜／甜點）。
I choose/order a drink/appetizer/dessert.

12 我們各點一道菜然後一起分享。
We each order a dish of our own and share it.

13 我掰開一雙筷子。
I split apart a pair of chopsticks.

14 我分配菜餚。
I dish out the food.

15 我使用牙籤。
I use a toothpick.

⑪ 「我們可以點餐了嗎？」說成 Can we order now?。
⑬ split apart 就是「分割（split）開（apart）」的意思。
⑭ 分菜也可改用 divide，例如 I divide salad into five plates.（我把沙拉分成 5 盤）。
⑰ 此句也可說成 make an additional order。

16 我叫住服務生。
I stop a <u>waiter</u>/<u>waitress</u>.

17 我加點另一道菜。
I make another order.

18 我把不喜歡的東西撥開。
I push aside what I don't care for.

19 我替每個人倒啤酒。
I go around pouring everyone beer.

20 我喝一杯。
I grab a drink.

⓲ push aside ~ 正如其字面，就是「把~推到旁邊」的意思。而 don't care for ~（不喜歡~）這種表達方式比 don't like ~ 有禮貌。
⓳「讓我為你倒啤酒吧？」就説成 Can I pour you some beer?。
⓴ 想問對方「下班後來去喝一杯如何？」時，可説成 What about a drink after work?。

21 我們各付各的。
We split the check.

22 我下載網路折價券並把它印出來。
I download an online coupon and print it out.

㉑ 此句也可說成 split the bill。而 go Dutch（各付各的）是較古老的說法，現在已不太使用。

㉒ 餐廳的折價券有時會標註 Coupon must be presented at time of order.（請於點菜時出示折價券）之類的注意事項。

利用電影或電視影集，製作專屬於你的原創句型集
武藤克彥 Text by Katsuhiko Muto

　　要能完全理解好萊塢電影或西洋影集中的英語，需要相當長的時間，不過在此讓我們改變一下觀點，傳授你一種將電影、影集中之表達方式內化的英語學習法。

1. 選擇內容與日常生活有關的電影、影集
不論內容多麼有趣，動作片中出現的那些台詞（e.g. I'm gonna kill you.）即使在一般中文對話裡也都用不到，故若欲學習日常生活的英語句型，最好選擇愛情喜劇或情境喜劇（situation comedy）。

2. 找出與自己年齡、性別接近的角色
就像在中文裡，男女老少的用字遣詞會略有不同，學習英語時也應模仿和自己同性別、同世代人物的英語表達方式。

3. 針對特殊部分做筆記
請先開啟中文字幕觀賞，碰到「嗯？這句的英語是什麼？這情況我也常遇到。」時，就暫停播放並切換成英文字幕，然後記下該句台詞或片語、詞彙。而若能以繪圖方式畫出動作或該情況，效果會更好。每部影片只需記下約 3 個部分就行了。請務必準備好筆記本，並將日期和影片名也記下來。

4. 利用數位相機
覺得做筆記很麻煩（It's a pain!）的人，可利用數位相機。就像我前幾天在影集中發現 Put your head back.（〔因流了很多鼻血所以〕請把頭往後仰）這個說法時，便利用了數位相機來記錄。因為我自己很討厭畫圖，所以就用數位相機把包含英文字幕的畫面給拍了下來。而只要將這類影像一一存進電腦，便能累積出你的「視覺化詞彙集」囉。

　　以上述方式利用電影或影集，便能一邊享受，一邊創造並累積專屬於自己的「英語句型集」。請務必一試！

1 ＜在餐廳＞天啊！顧客都排到店門外去了。
<At a restaurant> Gee! Customers are lining up out of the door.

2 這家餐廳人很多。他們說要等 40 分鐘。
The restaurant is very busy. They say the wait will be 40 minutes.

3 不接受初次來店的客人？真是有夠勢利！
No first-timers? How snobbish!

4 看來拉麵熱潮已經過了。
The ramen fad seems to have passed already.

5 真希望有一天我能到非迴轉的壽司店吃壽司。
I hope some day I can eat at a sushi bar where the dishes don't revolve.

6 有哪間燒肉店是可以讓我一個人進去吃的嗎？
Aren't there any yakiniku restaurants where I can eat alone?

Gee! = 表達驚訝之意的感嘆詞／customer = 顧客／line up = 排隊

「排隊等～」說成 wait in line for ~（美式）、wait in a queue for ~（英式）。例如 People have to wait in <u>line/a queue</u> for the ramen shop to open.（大家必須排隊等這家拉麵店開門）。

---

busy = 忙碌（生意很好）／wait（名詞）＝等待的時間

欲詢問餐廳「要等多久？」時，可使用名詞的 wait，說成 How long will the wait be?。若說 How long do we have to wait? 則聽起來有「到底要我們等多久？」這種抱怨的感覺。

---

first-timer = 初次到該店的人／snobbish = 勢利的

除了 How snobbish! 之外，也可說 What a nasty place!（這家店給人的感覺真差！）。而「踏進這間店需要一些勇氣」則說成 You've got to be brave to enter this restaurant.。

---

fad =〔一時的〕熱潮；流行／pass = 過去；消逝

而另一個字 boom 則是指「〔經濟等方面的〕快速成長、一時景氣」之意，例如 economic boom（經濟景氣），不同於 fad 所表達「熱潮、一時的流行」等意思。

---

some day = 有一天／revolve = 迴轉

「迴轉壽司」的英文可說成 belt-conveyor sushi 或 revolving sushi 等，不過其原始日語 kaitenzushi 現在也已相當普及。至於「〔有吧檯的〕壽司店」說成 sushi bar，吧檯就是 bar。

---

alone = 一個人；單獨

「被大家看到〔我一個人吃飯〕，而感到很不好意思」說成 Everyone's staring at me. It's embarrassing!。至於「專心用餐」則說成 Try to focus on eating.。

7 大阪燒和燒肉的缺點就是衣服會吸收氣味。
One bad thing about okonomi-yaki and yakiniku is that your clothes absorb the smell.

8 這家中菜館充滿了當地氣氛。
This Chinese restaurant is full of local atmosphere.

9 香煙的煙飄進了這裡的禁煙區。
The cigarette smoke is drifting over here into the non-smoking area.

10 請先給我咖啡就好。
Just coffee for now, please.

11 讓我們從啤酒喝起吧！
Let's start off with a beer!

12 嗯，我先看看菜單考慮一下。
Well, I'm just going to look over the menu and think about it.

absorb = 吸收

One bad thing about ~ is that... 就是「～的缺點之一便是……」之意。而其他使用了 thing 的句型還包括 The good thing is ~（好處是～）、The thing is ~（重點是～）、One bad thing happens after another.（禍不單行）等等。

---

local = 當地的；地方的／atmosphere = 氣氛

local是指「當地的、本地的」。「鄉下的」英文說成 rural、country，例如 I'd love to live a rural life.（我很嚮往鄉間生活）。

---

drift over ~ = 飄到～／non-smoking area（= smoke-free area）= 禁煙區

「隔板阻擋了煙，使之無法飄入禁煙區」說成 The partition prevents smoke from entering the smoke-free area.。 smoke-free 的 -free 就是「無～」的意思。

---

for now = 現在；目前 e.g. Bye for now. = 那麼再見囉

菜都點完後，欲補上一句「就先點這些吧」時，英語說成 That's it for now.。而還有人沒到，想說「先點一些飲料吧？」時，則說成 How about just ordering drinks first?。

---

start off with ~ = 從～開始；以～起頭

啤酒一般為不可數名詞，但若在 a glass of beer 等具有明確可數容器之狀況下，便能以可數名詞的方式 a beer (= a glass of beer) 來運用，例如 We ordered three beers each.（我們各點了 3 杯啤酒）。

---

look over ~ = 看一遍～

look over ~ 含有「瀏覽；檢閱」的意思，用法如 look over the papers（瀏覽文件）、look over a school（視察學校）等。

13 我在想到底該點什麼好，因為菜單上有太多不同的選擇了。
I wonder what to have, because there are so many choices on the menu.

14 光看菜單，我無法想像它的味道如何。
I can't imagine what it tastes like just by looking at the menu.

15 我可以點那個——隔壁桌那位老兄正在吃的菜嗎？
Can I have that — what the guy at the next table is having?

16 這個僅限於套餐嗎？
Is this one limited to the set course?

17 出菜真慢。也許我們點的單沒送到？
The food is taking a while. Maybe our order didn't go through.

18 這不是我們點的。
This is not what we ordered.

I wonder what to ~ = 我在想到底該～什麼好／choice = 選擇；選項

像這類「不知該選什麼」的情況，也可用 hesitate（猶豫）一詞來表達，例如 I hesitate over what to choose.。而若想進一步強調，則可說成 I'm at a loss about what to choose.（我無所適從，完全不知該選什麼好）。

imagine = 想像／taste like ~ = 味道像～

「英文菜單很難看懂」說成 It's hard to get a sense of the menu in English.，而「有中文的菜單嗎？」則說成 Do you have a menu in Chinese?。

at the next table = 隔壁桌的

在餐廳點菜時，「請給我～」可說成 Can I have ~?。若想要更有禮貌，就說 May I have ~?。而在速食店等，由店員直接把菜餚遞給顧客的情況下，大部分人會以 Can I get ~? 的句型來點菜，例如 Can I get a cheeseburger, please?（麻煩請給我一個起司漢堡）。

be limited to ~ = 限定於～／set course = 套餐；全餐

而「單品料理；單點」稱為 à la carte。例如 Why don't we pick something from the à la carte menu?（我們何不從單點的菜單裡挑選呢？）。

take a while = 需要一段時間／a while = 一段時間／go through =〔點的單〕送到〔廚師手上〕

當你點的菜過了很久都沒送上來時，便可說 Excuse me, my order hasn't come yet. I've been waiting for 15 minutes.（不好意思，我點的菜還沒來。我已經等了 15 分鐘）。

what S + V = 由 S 所 V 的東西

此例句也可說成 This is not what I asked for.。而若不很確定自己到底點了什麼時，則可說 I wonder if I ordered this one.（我懷疑我真的點了這個嗎？）。

19 我們沖昏了頭,點了太多。
We got carried away and ordered too much.

20 這是吃到飽的自助餐,但是你不該狼吞虎嚥。
This is an all-you-can-eat buffet, but you shouldn't pig out.

21 我不大懂什麼餐桌禮儀。
I don't know that much about table manners.

22 我就愛平民美食。
I just like everyday food.

23 我們使用刀叉時應該由外而內,不是嗎?
We should use the cutlery from the outside in, shouldn't we?

24 糟糕!我把它灑出來了!
Oh, shoot! I spilled it!

get carried away = 沖昏頭；得意忘形

「沖昏頭」也可說成 go overboard，例如 Don't go overboard.（別沖昏頭了）。

---

all-you-can-eat buffet = 吃到飽形式的自助餐／pig out = 狼吞虎嚥；大吃大喝

all-you-can-~ 就是「無限量～」的意思，例如 all-you-can-drink（無限暢飲）、all-you-can-sing（無限歡唱）。而「歐式自助餐」則叫 smorgasbord [ˈsmɔrɡəsˌbɔrd]。

---

table manners = 餐桌禮儀（manners 用複數形）

此例句也可改用 clue（線索）一詞，說成 I have no clue what table manners are.（我對餐桌禮儀一無所知）。

---

just = 就是／everyday food = 平常的食物

everyday 除了有「每天的」意思外，也包含「常見的；普通的」等意義（e.g. everyday clothes = 普通便服）。

---

cutlery = 刀叉餐具（刀、叉、湯匙等）

from the outside in 就是「由外而內」的意思，「由內而外」則說成 from the inside out。另外像 from the top down（由上而下）、from the bottom up（由下而上）等說法，也都很實用。

Oh, shoot! = 糟糕！／spill = 灑出

Oh, shoot! 是感嘆詞，表示「（出錯時說的）糟糕」之意。以此例的情況來說，也可用 Oops!（哎呀）。另外還有更強烈的說法，如 Damn!（可惡），但使用時須注意場所與對象。

25 很多食物你甚至沒試過就排斥不吃。

There are many foods you reject before even trying them.

26 這是我第一次吃到用這種方式烹調的章魚。

This is my first time eating octopus cooked like this.

27 這菜讓人想拿來配飯。

This food gives me a craving for steamed rice.

28 這道菜沒什麼味道。我覺得要再多點調味才好。

This has a bland taste. I think it needs more spice.

29 這間餐廳最近味道變差了。是因為換了主廚嗎？

This restaurant has lost its touch recently. Has the chef been replaced?

30 就其價格來說，這菜餚算是美味而且份量十足。我很滿意。

For its price, the food is tasty and there's a large amount. I'm so pleased.

reject = 排斥〔食物〕／try = 嘗試

「排斥而不吃～」可説成 reject ~ out of hand，例如 My brother rejects sashimi out of hand.（我哥哥排斥而不吃生魚片）。此處的 out of hand 是「想都不想」之意。

---

octopus = 章魚／cook = 烹調

「珍味」就説成 delicacy，例如 Octopus is regarded as a delicacy in some western countries.（在某些西方國家，章魚被視為珍味）、I want to try out all sorts of delicacies.（我想嚐遍所有珍味佳餚）。

---

craving for ~ = 渴望～／steam = 用蒸氣烹煮

「想吃～想到無法忍耐」可用誇張的動詞句型 kill for ~（願意為～而殺人）來表達，例如 I would kill for pizza now.（我現在想吃比薩想得受不了）。

---

bland =〔食物的味道〕淡而無味

bland 是指「味道淡」的意思，但「〔飲料〕沒味道」則用 vapid，如 vapid beer（無味的啤酒）。

---

touch = 技術；巧妙才能／recently = 最近／replace = 取代；替換

lose one's touch 就是「技術變差；退步」之意。而「維持技術水準」説成 keep one's touch，例如 He always tries to keep his touch as a chef.（他總是努力維持身為主廚的技術水準）。

---

tasty = 美味的；好吃的／amount = 份量／pleased = 心滿意足的；高興的

for ~ 是表示「就其～來説」之意的介系詞，如 The chef is highly-skilled for his age.（就其年齡而言，這位主廚的技術十分嫻熟）。

31 這裡的菜色齊備了三大要件：便宜、美味且份量十足。
The food here is a triple threat: cheap and tasty and lots of it.

---

32 此店的店員態度不佳，但是食物味道卻值得信賴。
The staff here are not very polite but you can rely on the food.

---

33 這裡的食物值得大排長龍等待。
This food is worth waiting in a long line for.

---

34 我是看了電視介紹之後才來的。不過它其實不怎麼樣。
I came here after seeing it on TV. It's no big deal, though.

---

35 很顯然地，這無法滿足我的食慾。
Apparently, it's not enough to fill my belly.

---

36 由於每盤菜的份量都很多，所以我吃不完。
I can't finish the food because there is too much on every plate.

triple = 三重的／threat = 威脅；構成威脅的人事物

注意，triple threat 其實是指「各要素皆齊備的人事物」之意，這裡的 threat 並無負面意義。而具負面意義的用法如 Do you really believe that smoking is not a threat to your health?（你真的相信抽煙對健康沒有威脅嗎？）。

---

staff = 員工（單數、複數形相同）／polite = 有禮貌的；殷勤的／rely on ~ = 倚賴~；信任~

「對~態度不好」可用 be impolite/not polite to ~。若用 a bad/poor attitude 則能表達更強烈的意思，例如 The waiter was fired because of his bad attitude.（那位服務生因其惡劣的態度而遭到開除）。

---

worth -ing = 值得~／in a long line = 大排長籠

「等候名單」就說成 waiting list，如 I should put down my name on the waiting list first.（我應該把我的名字寫進等候名單中）、Where am I on the waiting list?（我是等候名單中的第幾個？）。

---

big deal = 了不起的事／though = 不過；然而

It's no big deal. 就是「沒什麼大不了的；不怎麼樣」之意，比 It's not a big deal./It's not that big a deal.（並沒什麼了不得的）的意思更強烈些。

---

apparently = 顯然地／fill one's belly (= satisfy one's hunger) = 滿足食慾／belly = 肚子；胃

「〔食物的〕份量少」說成 small portion，例如 I wonder why they serve small portions in this restaurant.（我很好奇這餐廳為何提供這麼少份量的食物）。

---

finish (the food) = 吃完（食物）

「〔將食物〕一掃而空」可用 polish off 這個片語，例如 Wow, look how fast he polished off the plate!（哇，你看他好快就把整盤食物一掃而空了！）。

37 我吃了一大堆。
I've had plenty.

38 不知道這家餐廳是否可以外帶。
I wonder if this restaurant has some food to go.

39 我永遠都吃得下甜點的。
I always have room for dessert.

40 這間餐廳的氣氛很好。我得記住怎麼來才行。
This restaurant has a nice atmosphere. I'll have to remember how to get here.

41 今天的酒讓我好快就醉了。
The liquor's hit me so fast today.

42 既然大家都到齊了，就讓我們再乾一次杯吧！
Let's make another toast, as everyone's here now!

plenty = 大量

「我吃飽了」可說成 I'm full.。I've had enough. 則帶有「已經吃夠了，就到此為止吧」這類負面的意味，故使用時須特別注意。

---

wonder if ~ = 不知是否～（有疑問）／to go = 外帶（美式）

美國的速食店會問客人 For here or to go?（在這裡用還是帶走？），但在英國則通常說成 Eat here or take away?。

---

room = 餘地；空間

have room for ~ 就是「有容納～的空間」之意。而「留點肚子吃甜食」則說成 save some room for sweets.。

---

atmosphere = 氣氛／how to ~ = ～的方法

請特別注意，「〔場所的〕氣氛很好；很有氣氛」不可說成 This place is moody.，因 moody 是指「〔人〕喜怒無常」，例如 She is moody and sometimes hard to talk to.（她總是喜怒無常，有時很難溝通）。

---

liquor = 酒；烈酒（威士忌等）／hit ~ = 對～產生效果

「〔食物或飲料〕令人滿意；無可挑剔」可說成 hit the spot，例如 Cold beer hits the spot on a hot summer day, doesn't it?（炎炎夏日，冰啤酒最令人暢快滿足，不是嗎？）。

---

make a toast = 乾杯；敬酒

「乾杯」也可用 have a toast、raise one's glass 等片語來表達，而欲高呼「乾杯！」時，英語說成 Cheers!、Bottoms up! 等。另外「祝～」則說成 Here's to ~、To ~ 等，例如 Here's to your success. Cheers!（祝你成功。乾杯！）。

43 你喝完這杯酒就該停了吧？
Shouldn't you stop drinking with that one?

44 這家酒吧備有很多當地啤酒。我超愛！
This bar is well-stocked with local beers. I love it!

45 點一整瓶如何？
Ask for a bottle?

46 空腹喝烈酒是很危險的。
Strong <u>alcohol</u>/<u>booze</u> could be dangerous on an empty stomach.

47 在喝了一晚的酒後我們通常以一杯熱茶來收尾。
We usually end a night of drinking with a cup of hot tea.

48 你覺得換個地方如何？
What do you reckon we try another place?

stop ~ with ... = 到……為止不再～

Let's call it a night.（今晚就到此為止吧）不僅可用於工作結束時，也可用於飲酒聚餐的最後結尾。而主要用於工作方面的類似説法還有 Let's wrap it up.（我們就此〔工作或會議〕結束吧）。

---

be well-stocked with ~ = 備有豐富的～／local beer = 地方啤酒；當地啤酒

beer 用於敘述份量多寡時屬於不可數名詞（e.g. a lot of beer），但此例句描述的是啤酒的種類，故使用 beers。而「～的種類繁多」也可用 have a wide <u>selection/range</u> of ~、have a variety of ~ 等來表達。

---

ask for ~ = 點～；要求～

此例句為 Why don't we ask for a bottle? 或 How about asking for a bottle? 的簡略説法。在輕鬆隨興的會話中，經常會省略主詞與助動詞。

---

could = 有～的可能性（可能性比用 can 要低）／dangerous = 危險的

empty stomach 就是「空腹」之意，如 Deep-fried foods are heavy on an empty stomach.（油炸食物對空腹來説是很大的負擔）、You can't fight on an empty stomach.（餓著肚子是無法打仗的）。

---

end ~ = 結束～；替～收尾

「收尾；作結」還可用 finish 來表達，例如 I usually finish my lunch with a cup of coffee.（我通常都以一杯咖啡來結束午餐）。

---

reckon =認為

reckon 有「覺得如何」，的意思，例如 What do you reckon?（你覺得如何？）。而此例句也可説成 What do you say if we try another place?。

49 今天讓我請客吧。
Let me treat you today.

50 對不起。麻煩幫我結帳。
Excuse me. Can I have the bill, please?

51 聽說這家餐廳不收信用卡。
They say this restaurant doesn't take credit cards.

treat = 款待；請客

與「請客」相關的説法還有 I'll buy you lunch.（我請你吃午飯）、This dessert is on me.（這道甜點算我的）等。

---

bill = 結帳

「帳單」也可用 check 這個字，如 Check please.（請結帳）就是比較直截了當的講法，而 <u>Can</u> / <u>May</u> I have the check, please? 則較有禮貌。

---

take = 收／credit card = 信用卡

「可以用信用卡付帳嗎？」説成 Can I pay <u>with a</u> / <u>by</u> credit card?，或者你也可採用更有禮貌的説法是 Do you accept credit cards?（你們接受信用卡（付款）嗎？）。

Skit  外食篇 ————————————————

對宴會進行嚴格的事前檢查

Woman: **You think this place will be good for our party? It looks awful❶ from the outside.**

Man: **Come on❷. This Chinese restaurant is full of local atmosphere. You'll like it.**

W: **I don't know. I can't imagine what it tastes like just by looking at the menu.**

M: **Don't worry. The food here is a triple threat: cheap and tasty and lots of it.**

W: **You seem to be emphasizing❸ quantity❹ rather than quality.**

M: **Come on. Let's each order a dish of our own and share them.**

W: **I'd like a drink. I want to look over the wine list.**

M: **They don't have wine. But the bar is well-stocked with local beers. I love it!**

W: **I don't drink beer. And I can't split this pair of chopsticks apart.**

M: **I'll stop a waiter and get you❺ a new pair.**

W: **This is my first time eating octopus cooked like this. I don't think I like it.**

M: **What's wrong with it❻?**

W: **It's really bland. I think it needs more spice.**

M: **Are you finished❼ already?**

W: **I've had plenty.**

M: **You don't like it here, do you?**

W: **No, I don't. And I don't think our friends will either. How about trying another place?**

女子：你認為這是我們舉辦宴會的好地方嗎？外觀看來真是糟透了。

男子：別這樣。這家中菜館可是充滿了本地的氣息喔。你會喜歡的。

女：我不知道耶。光看菜單，我無法想像其味道如何。

男：別擔心，這裡的菜色齊備了三大要件：便宜、美味且份量十足。

女：你似乎重量不重質。

男：來吧。我們各點一道菜然後一起分享。

女：我想喝點什麼。我要看看酒單。

男：他們這裡沒有。不過吧檯備有很多當地啤酒，我超愛的！

女：我不喝啤酒。而且我掰不開這雙筷子。

男：我叫個服務生幫你換雙新的。

女：這是我第一次吃到用這種方式烹調的章魚。我不太喜歡。

男：有什麼不對嗎？

女：沒什麼味道。我覺得要再多點調味才好。

男：妳不吃了嗎？

女：我吃了一大堆。

男：妳不喜歡這間餐廳，對吧？

女：對，我不喜歡。而且我覺得我們的朋友也不會喜歡。何不找其他地方試試？

【單字片語】

❶ awful：極糟的；可怕的
❷ Come on.：別這樣。；來吧。
❸ emphasize：強調～；
❹ quantity：量；份量
❺ get you ～：幫你拿～
❻ What's wrong with ～?：～有什麼不對？
❼ ～ be finished：～完成了；～結束了

Quick Check

讓我們一起來複習本章所介紹過的句型！請依據以下中文句子的意思，來完成對應的英文句子。（答案就在本頁最下方。）

❶ 我盛裝打扮去高級餐廳用餐。→P196

I get ( ) ( ) ( ) and go to a ( ) restaurant.

❷ 我把不喜歡的東西撥開。→P199

I ( ) ( ) what I don't ( ) ( ).

❸ 不接受初次來店的客人？真是有夠勢利！→P202

No ( )? How ( )!

❹ 香煙的煙飄進了這裡的禁煙區。→P204

The cigarette smoke is ( ) ( ) here into the ( ) ( ).

❺ 我可以點那個——隔壁桌那位老兄正在吃的菜嗎？→P206

Can I ( ) that — what the guy ( ) ( ) ( ) ( ) is having?

❻ 我們沖昏了頭，點了太多。→P208

We ( ) ( ) ( ) and ( ) ( ) ( ).

❼ 這菜讓人想拿來配飯。→P210

This food ( ) ( ) a ( ) ( ) steamed rice.

❽ 很顯然地，這無法滿足我的食慾。→P212

Apparently, It's not ( ) ( ) ( ) ( ) ( ).

❾ 這間餐廳的氣氛很好。我得記住怎麼來才行。→P214

This restaurant ( ) ( ) ( ) ( ). I'll have to remember ( ) ( ) get here.

❿ 你喝完這杯酒就該停了吧？→P216

( ) you ( ) ( ) with ( ) ( )?

---

❶ all/dressed/up/classy ❷ push/aside/care/for ❸ first-timers/snobbish ❹ drifting/over/non-smoking/area ❺ have/at/the/next/table ❻ got/carried/away/ordered/too/much ❼ gives/me/craving/for ❽ enough/to/fill/my/belly ❾ has/a/nice/atmosphere/how/to ❿ Shouldn't/stop/drinking/that/one

chapter 9 Health & Diet

健康與飲食

現代人特別注重「身體健康」。
除了重視營養均衡之外，
更積極地做運動、努力瘦身與保養。
我們立刻開始學習各式工具及
方法的描述吧！

Words 單字篇

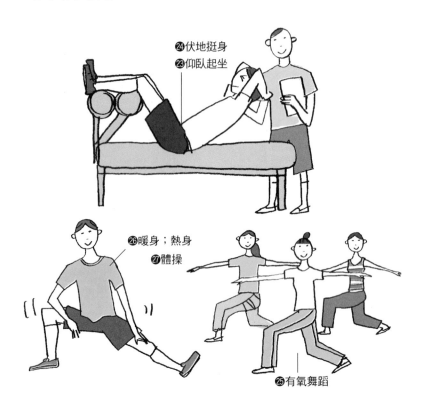

㉔伏地挺身
㉓仰臥起坐

㉖暖身；熱身
㉗體操

㉕有氧舞蹈

❶ scale　❷ chart　❸ clinical thermometer　❹ basal body temperature
❺ belly　❻ waist　❼ diet　❽ calorie　❾ weight rebound　❿ metabolism
⓫ basal metabolism　⓬ medical checkup　⓭ carbohydrate　⓮ protein

首先，讓我們透過各種物品的名稱，
來掌握「健康與飲食」給人的整體印象。

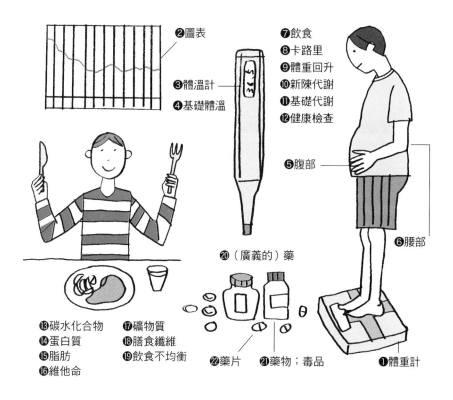

❷圖表
❸體溫計
❹基礎體溫
❼飲食
❽卡路里
❾體重回升
❿新陳代謝
⓫基礎代謝
⓬健康檢查
❺腹部
❻腰部
⓴（廣義的）藥
⓭碳水化合物
⓮蛋白質
⓯脂肪
⓰維他命
⓱礦物質
⓲膳食纖維
⓳飲食不均衡
㉒藥片
㉑藥物；毒品
❶體重計

⓯ fat ⓰ vitamine ⓱ mineral ⓲ dietary fiber ⓳ unbalanced diet
⓴ medicine ㉑ drug ㉒ tablet ㉓ sit-up ㉔ push-up ㉕ aerobics
㉖ warm-up ㉗ gymnastic exercise

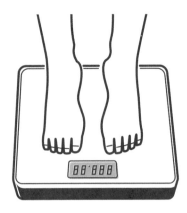

1 我用體重計量體重。
I weigh myself on the scale.

2 我把我的體重記錄成圖表。
I record my weight on a chart.

3 我嚐試流行／最新的節食方法。
I try <u>a popular</u> / <u>the latest</u> way of dieting.

4 我計算卡路里。
I count calories.

5 我消耗卡路里。
I burn off calories.

tips

❶ 「站上體重計」說成 get on the scale，而「體重是～公斤」說成 weigh ~ <u>kilograms/kilos</u>。另外，「體重增加（減少）」則用 gain (lose) weight。
❸ dieting 就是「節食」，而「進行節食」可說成 go on a diet。
❻ 這裡的 diet 是指「飲食；飲食習慣」，而 <u>high/rich</u> in ~ 則是「含豐富～的」之意。

6　我吃富含蛋白質的飲食。
I eat a diet <u>high</u> / <u>rich</u> in protein.

7　我減少碳水化合物的攝取。
I cut down on carbohydrates.

8　我少吃一餐。
I skip a meal.

9　我努力避免骨質疏鬆症。
I try to prevent bone loss.

10　我努力維持均衡的飲食。
I try to have a well-balanced diet.

❼ cut down on ~ 是「減少～」之意，而 carbohydrate（碳水化合物）可縮寫
　成 carb。「低碳水化合物飲食」就說成 low-carb diet。
❽ skip 是「略過～」之意。「絕食；斷食」說成 fast，而「戒掉甜食」則是
　<u>give up</u>/<u>stop</u> eating sweets。
❾ prevent 是「預防」之意，而「骨質疏鬆症」的正式名稱為 osteoporosis，
　唸成 [ɑstɪopə`rosɪs]。
❿「吃對身體有益的東西；吃得健康」就說成 eat healthy。

11 我加入運動俱樂部／健身房並定期去運動。
I join a <u>sports club</u> / <u>gym</u> and go there regularly.

12 我在跑步機上運動。
I work out on a treadmill.

13 我提高我的心跳速率。
I get my heart rate up.

14 我做伏地挺身。
I do push-ups.

15 我一邊看電視一邊做伸展運動。
I stretch while watching TV.

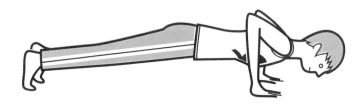

⑪「加入～」也可說成 become a member of ~。
⑭ do 這個動詞可用於各式各樣的運動，例如「做運動／有氧舞蹈／瑜珈／仰臥起坐／深蹲運動」就說成 do <u>exercise</u> / <u>aerobics</u> / <u>yoga</u> / <u>sit-ups</u> / <u>squats</u> 等。
⑰「上（下）樓梯」說成 <u>climb</u> / <u>go</u> up (down) the stairs。

16 我讓自己冷靜下來。
I cool down.

17 我不用手扶梯或電梯，而改爬樓梯。
Instead of using escalators or elevators, I try to use the stairs.

18 我利用工作空檔運動。
I exercise in my spare moments from work.

19 我提早一站下車然後走過去。
I get off at the <u>station</u> / <u>stop</u> before mine and walk.

20 我不坐車而是騎腳踏車通勤。
I commute by bicycle instead of by car.

⓲ spare 是「剩下的；備用的」之意，故 in one's spare moments 就表示「空閒時；閒暇時」的意思。
⓳ 「快走」說成 brisk walking，而「計步器」是 pedometer [pɪˋdɑmətə]。
⓴ commute 為「通勤」之意，而「騎腳踏車上班」說成 ride a bicycle to work。

21 我維持規律的生活。
I keep regular hours.

22 我正確地洗手並漱口。
I wash my hands and gargle properly.

23 我站直身子。
I stand up straight.

24 我記錄自己的飲食狀況。
I keep a record of what I eat.

25 我記錄我的基礎體溫。
I keep a record of my basal body temperature.

tips

㉑ 相反地,「不規律的生活」則說成 keep irregular hours。
而「早睡早起」是 keep early hours,「熬夜」是 keep late hours。

㉓ 「坐直身子」說成 sit up straight,而「駝背」則可說成 hunch over。

26 我接受流感（疫苗）注射
I get a flu shot.

27 我接受完整的健康檢查。
I get <u>a thorough medical examination</u> / <u>a complete medical checkup</u>.

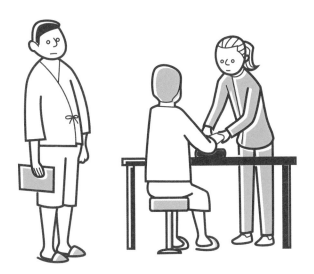

❷❹ keep a record of ~ 就是「記錄～」。

❷❻ flu 就是 influenza（流行性感冒），shot 為「注射；打針」之意，而「流感疫苗」為 flu vaccine。

❷❼ medical checkup 就是「健康檢查」。「定期健檢」可說成 routine physical [examination]，而「接受定期健檢」則說成 get regular [medical] check-ups。

1 我穿不下前一陣子所買的褲子。
I can't fit in the pants I bought a while ago.

2 隨著年齡增加，我們身體的新陳代謝會減緩。
Our body's metabolism slows down as we get older.

3 首先，我必須提高我的基礎代謝。
First of all, I have to increase my basal metabolism.

4 真是抱歉了，我竟然這麼胖！
Excuse me for being so fat!

5 我從明天開始節食！
I'll go on a diet starting tomorrow!

6 我想在穿泳裝的季節來臨前減掉至少 3 公斤。
I want to lose at least three kilograms before the swimsuit season.

fit in ~ = 可穿上～／a while ago = 前一陣子

「我的衣服變得不合身了」可說成 My clothes don't fit me anymore.，而「太緊」則用 be too tight 來表達，如 This <u>skirt</u> / <u>jacket</u> is too tight.。

---

metabolism =〔新陳〕代謝 cf. metabolic syndrome = 代謝症候群／slow down = 速度減緩／as we get older = 隨著我們年齡增長

---

first of all = 第一；首先／increase = 增加／basal metabolism = 基礎代謝

基礎代謝是指人不動時也會消耗的熱量。而「我應該消耗更多卡路里才行」說成 I should burn more calories.。

---

excuse me for ~ =〈語帶諷刺地〉對～我深感抱歉／fat = 胖的 cf. overweight = 過重的／obese = 肥胖的

此例句也可說成 Yeah, I'm overweight, and so what?（是啊，我過重，那又怎樣？）。

---

go on a diet = 進行節食／starting tomorrow = 明天開始

「節食中」說成 on a diet，故「我正在節食」就說成 I'm on a diet.。另外，「注意監控體重的人」說成 weight-watcher。

---

at least = 至少／swimsuit (= <u>bathing suit</u> / <u>swimwear</u>) = 泳裝

各種泳裝的英文名稱如下：one-piece swimsuit（連身式泳裝）、bikini（比基尼）、<u>swimshorts</u> / <u>swim trunks</u>（泳褲）。

7　沒有喝了就能減重的飲料這種東西。

There is no such thing as a weight-loss drink.

8　走兩個小時的路才能燃燒掉相當於一小塊蛋糕的卡路里…真是白搭！

Two hours' walking burns the same amount of calories as a tiny piece of cake ... so futile!

9　我無法抗拒甜食的誘惑。

I can't resist eating sweets.

10　我腰部周圍的贅肉為何如此難以擺脫？

Why is it so difficult to get rid of the fat around my waist?

11　大腿實在很難瘦下來。

It's not easy to lose weight off my thighs.

12　我體重馬上就回升了。

I put the weight back on in no time.

There is no such thing as ~ = 沒有～這種東西／weight-loss = 減重 cf. weight-gain = 增重

此例句也可說成 There is nothing that will make you <u>thin</u> / <u>lose weight</u> just by drinking it!。

---

a tiny piece of ~ = 很小的一塊～ cf. a slice of cake = 一片蛋糕／futile = 無益的；徒勞的

so futile 在此指再努力也沒意義。

---

resist = 抗拒／sweets (= sweet things) = 甜食

此例句也可說成 I can't stop myself from eating sweets.（我無法阻止自己不吃甜食）。而「嗜吃甜食」說成 have a sweet tooth，「吃零食」則說成 have a snack。

---

get rid of ~ = 去除～／fat = 脂肪（贅肉）／around one's waist = 腰部周圍的 cf. around my belly = 腹部周圍的

「甩掉多餘體重」說成 get rid of extra weight，而一般俗稱的「游泳圈；鮪魚肚」可說成 spare tire（備胎）。

---

lose weight off ~ (= get the weight off ~) = 減少～的重量／thigh = 大腿 cf. calf（複數形為 calves）= 小腿肚／knee = 膝蓋

請注意，腳踝以上的部分稱為 leg（腿），腳踝以下的部分稱為 foot（腳；複數形為 feet）。而「腳踝」則叫 ankle。

---

put the weight on (= gain weight) = 體重增加／in no time = 馬上；立刻

若欲表達「體重再度增加」之意，可說成 I regained the weight.。而減重之後的「體重回升」說成 weight rebound。rebound 這個字單獨使用時，意思為「反彈」。

13 她減重後簡直判若兩人！
She has lost some weight and now looks so different!

14 最近我的腰瘦了約 2 個皮帶孔的大小。
My belt is two holes smaller these days.

15 我的衣服得全部重買了！
I must replace all my old clothes with new ones!

16 我的體形日漸鬆弛。
My figure is getting flabby.

17 我的腰部越來越胖！
I'm getting fat around the waist!

18 我想鍛鍊身體！
I want to tone up my body!

lose weight = 體重減少 cf. become thin = 變瘦／look different = 看起來不一樣

此例句也可説成 I hardly recognized her because she became thin.（我幾乎認不出她來，因為她變瘦了）。

若想具體表達「腰部瘦了～公分」，則可説成 I lost ~ centimeters off my waist.。

---

replace ~ with ... = 用……取代～

此例句中的 ones 為代名詞，指 clothes。

---

figure = 體形；身材 e.g. have a good figure = 身材姣好／flabby = 鬆弛；不結實

「我的身材漸漸走樣」就説成 I'm losing my shape.

---

get fat = 發胖／around the waist = 腰部周圍

此例句直譯為中文便是「我的腰部周圍發胖了」，也可説成 I have no waist!（我沒有腰！）。

---

tone up ~ =使～健壯；使～緊實

tone 為動詞，有「調整～狀況」的意思。而「雕塑體形」説成 get in shape，「緊實的／沒有贅肉的身體」則説成 trim / lean body。

19 我得多增強我的肌肉才行。
I need to build up my muscles a little.

20 我從沒想過體操竟然是這麼累人。
I'd never have imagined gymnastic exercises would wear me out.

21 仰臥起坐對你的腰痛會有效。
Sit-ups will work for your backache.

22 我最近不常去健身房。
Lately, I don't go to the gym very often.

23 我不太願意參加有氧舞蹈課程，因為其他的學員都是女生。
I hesitate to join the aerobics lessons, because all the other members are women.

24 我做了太多運動，現在腰很痛。
I did too much exercise and now my back hurts.

build up ~ = 增強～／muscle = 肌肉 cf. muscular = 肌肉發達的；健壯的

「健身」叫 body building，「重量訓練」則叫 weight training。

I'd never have imagined = 我從沒想過／gymnastic exercises = 體操 cf. calisthenics [ˌkæləsˈθɛnɪks] = 健美操／wear ~ out (= make ~ tired) = 使～疲累

注意，wear 的過去式為 wore，過去分詞是 worn。

---

sit-up = 仰臥起坐／work for ~ = 對～有效／backache (= back pain) = 腰、背的疼痛

此例句也可說成 Sit-ups will ease your backache.（仰臥起坐能減緩你的腰痛）。英文裡描述腰痛的「腰」時，並無特殊單字可用，通常都用 back 或 lower back 來表示。

---

lately (= these days) = 最近／go to the gym = 上健身房

「我沒去上我的健身房課程」可說成 I skip my gym classes.。一般會話中較常用 gym（健身房）一詞，較少用 sports club（運動俱樂部）。

---

hesitate = 遲疑；猶豫／aerobics = 有氧舞蹈

此例句中 because 之後的部分也可說成 because I'm the only guy / man in the group（因為我是群體中唯一的男生）。

---

do exercise = 做運動／do too much ~ = 做太多～／hurt = 痛

「我腰酸背痛」就說成 My back is sore / in pain.。

25 你沒暖身，難怪腿會抽筋。

You didn't do a warm-up. No wonder you got a cramp in your leg.

26 我想我老了。運動之後我全身肌肉痠痛。

I guess I'm getting old. I have sore muscles all over my body after the exercise.

27 我大部分時間都坐在桌前工作，所以運動量太少。

I get too little exercise because I work sitting at a desk most of the time.

28 我總是外食，所以一天要攝取 30 種食材是不可能的。

I always eat out, so it's impossible to get 30 ingredients a day.

29 自從我開始採取以日本料理為主的飲食之後，膽固醇指數就下降了！

My cholesterol level dropped since I began eating mainly Japanese food.

30 由於飲食不均衡，所以我現在有貧血問題。

Because of my unbalanced diet, I now have anemia.

warm-up (= warm-up exercises) = 暖身運動／No wonder ~ = 難怪會~／cramp = 抽筋；痙攣／get a cramp in one's leg = 腿抽筋 cf. get a cramp in the calf = 小腿抽筋

此例的第二句也可說成 That's why you got a cramp in your leg.（這就是為什麼你的腿會抽筋）。

---

guess = 猜想；覺得／sore muscles = 肌肉痠痛／sore = 疼痛的／all over one's body = 全身

「我筋肉痠痛」可說成 My muscles <u>are sore</u> / <u>ache</u>.

---

too little ~ = ~太少／most of the time = 大部分時間 cf. all day = 整天

「文書工作」就是 desk work，而「坐在辦公桌前工作」則說成 work at one's desk。

---

eat out = 外食／ingredient = 成分；食材 cf. food items = 食品項目

「每天吃~種項目的食品」也可說成 eat ~ food items every day。而「自己下廚」則可說成 <u>cook</u> / <u>fix</u> / <u>prepare</u> one's own meals、do one's own cooking、cook at home 等。

---

cholesterol [kə`lɛstə͵rol] level = 膽固醇指數／drop (= lower) = 下降／Japanese food = 日本料理

「〔血液中的〕膽固醇高」就說成 have high [blood] cholesterol level。而「高血壓」是 high blood pressure，「高血糖」是 high blood sugar，「中性脂肪」則是 neutral fat。

---

unbalanced diet = 不均衡的飲食／anemia = 貧血

「我很挑食」說成 I am a picky eater.，而「我因貧血而頭暈目眩」則可說成 I get dizzy from the lack of blood.

31 我現在的體力沒以前那麼好了。
I don't have as much energy as I used to.

32 以前，我可以整晚熬夜一直工作到隔天。
In the past, I could stay up all night and work through to the next day.

33 生理痛真是痛死我了。
My cramps are killing me.

34 我的眼睛好累。
My eyes are weary.

35 我想我感冒了，所以我會吃些藥然後上床睡覺。
I think I'm getting a cold, so I'll take some medicine and go to bed.

36 我想改善健康狀況，變得不再過敏。
I want to improve my health and become allergy-free.

energy = 能量；活力／as much ~ as ... = 和……一樣的～

也可説成 I don't have as much strength as I did.（我的力氣已大不如前）。

---

in the past = 以前／stay up all night = 整晚熬夜

此例句也可説成 I used to stay up all night and work through to the next day.。「徹夜工作」是 work <u>overnight</u> ／ <u>through the night</u>，而「熬夜工作／徹夜苦讀」則有種特別説法，那就是 burn the midnight oil。

---

cramps（= menstrual cramps）= 生理痛 cf. cramp = 抽筋；痙攣／kill ~ = 使～痛得受不了 e.g. My feet are killing me. = 我的腳痛得要命

此例句也可説成 I'm suffering from severe menstrual pains.（我因嚴重的生理痛而痛苦不堪）。而「我生理痛」就説成 I've got cramps.。

---

weary = 疲勞 cf. eyestrain =〔因過度使用造成的〕眼睛疲勞

本句也可用 tired 取代 weary。「揉一揉疲倦的眼睛」可説成 rub one's <u>tired</u> / <u>weary</u> eyes。

---

be getting a cold = 感冒了／take medicine = 吃藥／medicine =〔最廣義的〕藥 cf. drug = 藥物；毒品／pill = 藥丸／tablet = 藥片／capsule = 膠囊

注意，欲表達「吃藥」之意時，動詞要用 take。

---

improve one's health = 增進健康狀況／allergy-free = 不過敏／~-free = 不～

請注意 allergy 的發音為［ˈælədʒɪ］。「擺脱我的過敏症」可説成 get rid of my allergy。

37 無論有多忙，我都應該接受健康檢查。
I should get a medical checkup no matter how busy I am.

38 保持健康是最重要的事。
Staying healthy is the most important thing.

medical checkup (= medical examination) = 健康檢查／no matter how ~ = 無論有多~

「徹底檢查」說成 thorough <u>checkup</u> / <u>examination</u>。另，「接受治療」說成 <u>get</u> / <u>undergo</u> [medical] treatment。

---

stay healthy (= <u>stay well</u> / <u>keep one's good health</u>) = 維持健康／the most important ~ = 最重要的~

此例句也可說成 There is nothing more valuable than good health.（沒有什麼比健康更有價值）。

這樣是瘦不了的!

Woman: **Wow, Bob! I haven't seen you in a while❶. You've lost some weight and you look so different.**

Man: **Thanks for noticing! I couldn't fit into the pants I bought a while ago, so I joined a gym and go there regularly now.**

W: **I get too little exercise because I work sitting at a desk all day. But after work I'm too tired to❷ go to the gym.**

M: **There are other things you can do. Instead of escalators or elevators, try to use stairs.**

W: **Climbing stairs makes my back hurt❸.**

M: **Sit-ups will work for your back pain.**

W: **I hate sit-ups!**

M: **Well, when you go home, get off at the stop before yours and walk.**

W: **Did you know two hours' walking burns the same amount of calories as a tiny piece of cake? It's useless.**

M: **But staying healthy is the most important thing.**

W: **I weigh myself on the scale every morning. And I count calories. If I gain some weight❹, I cut down on carbs or skip meals.**

M: **That won't work❺ forever. Your body's metabolism will slow down as you get older.**

W: **Are you saying I'm getting old?**

女性：哇，鮑伯！好一陣子沒看到你。你瘦了，簡直是判若兩人。

男性：真謝謝妳有注意到！我穿不下前一陣子所買的褲子，所以就加入了健身房，現在我都定期去運動。

女：因為我整天都坐在辦公桌前工作，所以運動量太少。可是下班後又累得無法上健身房。

男：還有其他的做法啊。妳可以試著不用手扶梯或電梯，改爬樓梯。

女：爬樓梯會造成我腰痛。

男：仰臥起坐對腰痛很有效喔。

女：我討厭仰臥起坐！

男：嗯，那妳回家的時候可以提早一站下車然後走回去。

女：你知道走兩個小時的路才能燃燒掉相當於一小塊蛋糕的卡路里嗎？這是白費力氣。

男：可是保持健康是最重要的。

女：我每天早上都用體重計量體重。我還計算卡路里。如果體重增加了，我就減少碳水化合物的攝取，或少吃幾餐。

男：這種方式不會一直有效的。妳身體的新陳代謝速度會隨著年齡增長而減緩。

女：你的意思是我老了？

【單字片語】

❶ I haven't seen you in a while.：好一陣子沒看到你了。

❷ too tired to～：太疲累以至於無法～

❸ make ～ hurt：使～疼痛

❹ gain weight：增加體重

❺ work：有效；有用

Quick Check

讓我們一起來複習本章所介紹過的句型！請依據以下中文句子的意思，來完成對應的英文句子。（答案就在本頁最下方。）

❶ 我吃富含蛋白質的飲食。**→P227**

I eat a diet ( ) ( ) ( ).

❷ 我做伏地挺身。**→P228**

I ( ) ( ).

❸ 我利用工作空檔運動。**→P229**

I ( ) ( ) ( ) ( ) ( ) from work.

❹ 我記錄我的基礎體溫。**→P230**

I ( ) ( ) ( ) ( ) my ( ) ( ) temperature.

❺ 首先，我必須提高我的基礎代謝。**→P232**

( ) ( ) ( ), I have to increase my ( ) ( ).

❻ 我腰部周圍的贅肉為何如此難以擺脫？**→P234**

Why is it so ( ) to ( ) ( ) ( ) the fat around my waist?

❼ 我想鍛鍊身體！**→P236**

I want to ( ) ( ) my body!

❽ 我做了太多運動，現在腰很痛。**→P238**

I ( ) ( ) ( ) exercise and now ( ) ( ) ( ).

❾ 你沒暖身，難怪腿會抽筋。**→P240**

You didn't ( ) ( ) ( ). ( ) ( ) you got a ( ) in your leg.

❿ 我的眼睛好累。**→P242**

( ) ( ) are ( ).

---

❶ high (rich)/in/protein ❷ do/push-ups ❸ exercise/in/my/spare/moments ❹ keep/a/record/of/basal/body ❺ First/of/all/basal/metabolism ❻ difficult/get/rid/of ❼ tone/ up ❽ did/too/much/my/back/hurts ❾ do/a/warm-up/No/wonder/cramp ❿ My/eyes/weary

夜晚

本章介紹夜晚回到家至就寢這段時間
可用的各種句型。
在換衣服、保養皮膚、準備就寢等
例行動作的同時，你可能陷入沉思，
也可能開始思考明天要做的事。
就讓我們一起看看在一天結束時，
有哪些表達方式可以描述這些讓人靜下
心來的動作，以及突然浮上心頭之思緒。

Words 單字篇

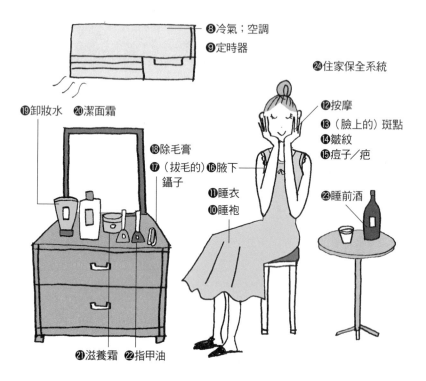

❽冷氣；空調
❾定時器
㉔住家保全系統
⑲卸妝水　⑳潔面霜
⑫按摩
⑬（臉上的）斑點
⑭皺紋
⑮痘子／疤
⑱除毛膏
⑰（拔毛的）⑯腋下
鑷子
⑪睡衣
⑩睡袍
㉓睡前酒
㉑滋養霜　㉒指甲油

❶ bathtub　❷ bubble bath　❸ facial mask　❹ shampoo　❺ conditioner
❻ bath powder　❼ shower gel　❽ air conditioner　❾ timer
❿ nightgown　⓫ nightwear　⓬ massage　⓭ blemish　⓮ wrinkle

首先，讓我們透過各種物品的名稱，
來掌握「夜晚」給人的整體印象。

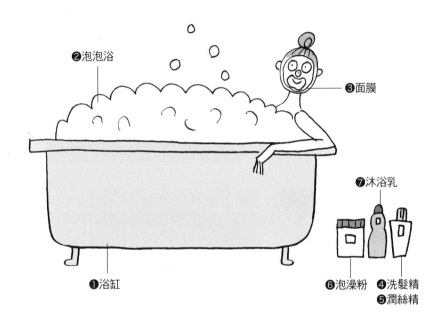

❷泡泡浴

❸面膜

❼沐浴乳

❻泡澡粉　❹洗髮精
❺潤絲精

❶浴缸

❶ pimple/spot　❶ armpit　❶ tweezer　❶ hair-removing cream
❶ makeup remover　❷ cleansing cream　❷ nourishing cream
❷ nail polish　❷ nightcap　❷ home security system

1 我打開前門的鎖。
I unlock the front door.

2 我開燈。
I turn on the lights.

3 我拿下領帶。
I take off my tie.

4 我把外套掛起來。
I hang up my jacket.

5 我卸妝。
I take off my makeup.

tips

❸ take off 是指把穿在身上的東西「取下；脫掉」，舉凡 clothes（衣服）、shoes（鞋子）、glasses（眼鏡）、contact lenses（隱形眼鏡）等等都可使用此動詞。

❺「卸妝水」之類的用品說成 makeup remover，而「用潔面霜卸妝」則說成 wipe off one's makeup with cleansing cream。

6 我吃晚飯配杯酒。
**I have a drink
with my dinner.**

7 我預先準備明天的晚餐。
**I prepare in advance
for tomorrow's dinner.**

8 我看今天的報紙。
I read today's paper.

9 我檢查小孩的功課。
I check my child's homework.

10 我決定明天要穿什麼衣服。
I decide what to wear for tomorrow.

❼ prepare in advance 就是「事先準備」之意。
❽ today's paper 指「今天的報紙」，paper 為 newspaper 的簡化。
❾「協助小孩做功課」說成 help with one's child's homework。
❿「選擇明天要穿的衣服」說成 pick out one's clothes for tomorrow。

11 我將洗澡水加熱。
I heat the bath water.

12 我用洗髮精洗頭。
I shampoo my hair.

13 我做半身浴。
I soak waist-down in a bathtub.

14 我擦乾我的身體。
I dry my body.

15 我吹乾我的頭髮。
I blow-dry my hair.

tips

⓫ 「加熱洗澡水」並不會把水煮到滾，所以不用 boil 這個動詞。而「清洗浴缸」說成 clean the bathtub，「放熱水到浴缸裡」則說成 <u>fill the bath</u> / <u>fill in the bathtub</u> with hot water。
⓬ 「沖洗頭髮」說成 rinse one's hair，而「潤絲」則要說 put conditioner on one's hair。「潤絲精」就是 [hair] conditioner。

16 我妥善照顧我的身體。
I take good care of my body.

17 我替自己排毒。
I detox myself.

18 我刮除腋下（手臂／腿部）的毛。
I shave my armpits (<u>arms</u> / <u>legs</u>).

19 我按摩我的頭皮。
I massage my scalp.

20 我把清除粉刺的貼布貼在鼻子上。
I apply a pack to my nose.

⓭ waist-down 是指「腰部以下」，而「泡腳；洗腳」説成 footbath。
⓰「仔細照顧身體」也可説成 look after one's body carefully。
⓲ armpit 是「腋下」。「除毛」説成 remove one's hair；「使用除毛膏」説成 use hair-removing cream；「用鑷子拔眉毛」則是 pluck one's eyebrows with tweezers。

21 我為小孩唸睡前床邊故事。
I read a bedtime story to my child.

23 我打開空調的定時器。
I turn on the timer for the air conditioner.

22 我熬夜。
I stay up late.

24 我上床〔準備睡覺〕。
I get into bed.

tips

㉑ bed time 指「上床〔就寢〕時間」，bedtime story 即「床邊故事」。另外，「童話」則説成 fairy tale。而「我哄小孩睡覺」則是 I put my child to bed.。

㉒ stay up〔late〕就是「熬夜」，而「徹夜不睡」則是 stay up all night。

㉔ get into bed 是「上床」之意，而 go to bed 則是「上床睡覺」。

練習運用例句來讓會話更順暢
荒井 貴和 Text by Kiwa Arai

要讓會話順暢的關鍵有二：（一）說出自己想說的、（二）充分理解對方說的話並做出適當回應。以下，便為各位介紹能實現這兩個關鍵的練習方法。

1. 為了能「說出自己想說的」

這部分可以一個人單獨練習。請將本書中與你自身經驗、感覺相符的句型記起來，並嘗試運用。與其不加思考地進行機械式練習，不如將情境套用到自己身上，經思考後再把話說出來，如此較容易記牢。

至於那些不適用於自己的句型，有兩種方法可以活用。一種方法是依據自身狀況來修改例句。例如，若你不是「坐火車」而是「坐公車」，那就把 I get on the train. 改成 I get on the bus.。另一種方式則是假裝自己是虛構人物。例如，你本身並非上班族，也不是家庭主婦，但是你可想像自己是上班族或家庭主婦，再嘗試運用該句型。這樣不僅能拓展你的表達能力範圍，也能幫助你理解別人說的話。

2. 為了能「充分理解對方說的話並做出適當回應」

在有對象存在的會話情境中，以順暢的節奏相互回應讓會話不中斷是很重要的。當你無法立刻說出想說的話時，可利用 Uh.../Well.../Let me see... 等來爭取思考時間。

此外，將本書所列之例句改成問句，便能向對方提出各式各樣的問題（例如，I check my fortune on TV. → Do you check your fortune on TV?）。而被對方問問題時，千萬別用 Yes 或 No 一個字就答完，最好能多加說明（"Do you go to the gym?" "Yes, at least once a week."）或反問對方（And you?/How about you?），這樣會話才能繼續下去。聆聽對方發言時，也該適度地搭腔（Uh-huh./Is that so?/Right./I see.）或以動作回應（點頭等），以表示你有認真在聽。而有時重複對方所說的話，或其話中的某個部分（例如，對方若說 "I do the gardening."，你便可以問他／她 "Oh, the gardening?/You do the gardening?"）也很有效果。

1 嗨，塔瑪！你今天有乖嗎？
Hi, Tama! Were you a good girl today?

2 又過了午夜！
It's past midnight again!

3 糟糕！我沒鎖門！
Oh no! I left the door unlocked!

4 我離開時忘了關掉空調。
I forgot to turn off the air conditioner when I left.

5 有個從家鄉寄來的包裹今天應該會送到！
A package from my hometown should arrive today!

6 節目是否都有錄到？
Has the program been recorded all right?

good girl = 好女孩 cf. bad girl = 壞女孩／naughty girl = 頑皮的女孩（若是男生，當然就改用 boy）

「要乖喔」就説成 Be a good <u>girl</u> / <u>boy</u>.。

---

past = 超過／midnight = 午夜；半夜十二點 cf. at a late (an early) hour = 深夜（清晨）時刻／wee hours [of the morning] = 凌晨

「我過了午夜才回家」就説成 I came home after midnight.。

---

left < leave = 留下～的狀態／unlocked = 未上鎖的 cf. unlock = 打開～的鎖／lock = 鎖上（<u>lock</u> / <u>unlock</u> the door = 鎖上／打開門鎖）

「我忘了鎖門！」就説成 I forgot to lock the door!。

---

forget to ～ = 忘了做～／turn off ～ = 關掉～；關閉～ cf. turn on ～ = 打開～／left < leave = 離開

此例句也可説成 I left the air conditioner on and went out.（我沒關空調就出去了），但其中的 left (leave) 與例句 3 的 left 意義相同，而 leave ～ on 便是「讓一直開著～」之意。

---

package = 包裹／hometown = 故鄉；家鄉

should 是「應該會」之意。此例句也可説成 I'm supposed to receive a package from my hometown today.（我今天應該會收到一個家鄉寄來的包裹）。

---

record = 錄 e.g. record a TV program = 錄電視節目／all right = 正確地；順利地

「預約錄影」説成 <u>timer</u> / <u>programmed</u> recording，而「用遙控器跳過廣告」則説成 skip commercials with the remote。

7　我有點餓了。
I'm a little bit hungry.

8　我要吃泡麵當宵夜。
I'm going to eat instant noodles for a midnight snack.

9　我會用微波爐把這個加熱來當晚餐吃。
I'll microwave this for my dinner.

10　最近我的皮膚開始變得乾燥。
Recently my skin has started drying out.

11　噢，我這裡竟然有個斑點。
Oh, I've found a blemish here.

12　我該怎麼做才能撫平這些皺紋呢？
What should I do to smooth this wrinkle?

a little bit = 有一點點

「我肚子餓扁了」說成 I'm <u>starving</u> / <u>starved</u>!；「我飽了」可說成 I'm <u>stuffed</u> / <u>full</u>.；「我的肚子餓得咕咕叫」則是 My stomach's growling.。

---

instant noodles = 泡麵 cf. noodles = 麵條／buckwheat noodles = 蕎麥麵／wheat noodles (udon) = 烏龍麵／Chinese noodles = 中式麵條／fried [Chinese] noodles = 〔中式〕炒麵／snack = 點心；零食

若是吃杯裝泡麵，也可說成 I'll have a cup noodle for a late-night snack.。

---

microwave = 用微波爐加熱 cf. stove = 火爐／oven = 烤箱／toaster oven = 烤麵包機

microwave [oven] 指「微波爐」，故「將～放進微波爐（加熱）」就說成 put (heat) ~ in the microwave [oven]。

---

dry out = 變得乾燥粗糙

「皮膚乾燥」說成 dry skin；而「肌膚光滑」說成 smooth skin；「肌膚緊緻彈性」說成 <u>firm</u> / <u>supple</u> skin；「滋潤肌膚」則是 moisturize one's skin。

---

blemish = 斑點；傷疤 cf. blotch = 疙瘩／freckles = 雀斑

欲表達「在臉部（額頭／臉頰／下巴）…」之類具體位置時，可將此例句中的 here 改成 on my face (forehead/cheek/chin)。

---

wrinkle = 皺紋 cf. lines (= creases) around one's mouth = 嘴邊的皺紋／crow's feet = 魚尾紋／smooth a wrinkle = 撫平皺紋

此例句也可說成 Can't I do anything to remove this wrinkle? 其中的 remove 指「除去」。

13 我們的皮膚是從幾歲開始會出現老化徵兆？
At what age does our skin start showing signs of aging?

14 這些痘子不太容易消除。
These pimples don't go away easily.

15 我的腳浮腫得好厲害。
My feet are badly swollen.

16 我的頭髮損傷得很嚴重。我這個週末得去一趟美容院才行。
My hair is badly damaged. I have to go to the beauty shop this weekend.

17 我今晚要用好的泡澡粉來款待自己。
I'm going to use a nice bath powder as a treat for myself tonight.

18 舒服地泡個澡真是令人神清氣爽。
It's so refreshing to soak in a bath comfortably.

start showing signs of ~ = 開始出現～的徵兆／aging = 老化（名詞）cf. age = 變老（動詞）／aging society = 高齡化（形容詞）社會

此例句也可説成 When is the turning point for our skin?，而其中的 turning point 就是指「轉捩點；轉折點」。

---

pimple (= spot) = 痘子；疤 cf. spot cream = 治療痘子用的面霜／pock mark = 痘疤／concealer = 遮瑕膏／go away = 消失／easily = 輕易地

此例句也可説成 I can't get rid of these pimples. 其中的 get rid of 指「清除」。

---

feet < foot = 腳／badly = 嚴重地／swollen = 浮腫的；膨脹的 e.g. swollen hand (leg) = 浮腫的手（腳）／swell = 腫脹；使～膨脹

「我的腳因為站了一整天而腫脹」説成 My feet are swollen [up] from standing all day.，而「我的雙腿無力」則説成 My legs feel heavy.。

---

badly = 嚴重地／damage = 損傷／beauty shop (= beauty parlor / beauty salon / hair salon) = 美容院 cf. barber shop = 理髮店

「我的頭髮變少了」説成 My hair is thinning.。而「剪頭髮」説成 get / have a haircut 或 get / have one's hair cut；「燙頭髮」説成 have one's hair permed；「染頭髮」則是 dye one's hair 或 get / have one's hair colored。

---

bath powder = 泡澡粉 cf. bubble bath = 泡泡浴／shower gel = 沐浴乳／treat = 款待

此例句也可説成 I'm going to use a good bath powder as a reward to myself tonight.。而「在浴缸裡放進泡澡粉」就説成 put some bath powder in the bathtub。

---

refreshing = 提神的；清爽的／soak = 浸泡

此例句也可説成 It's so refreshing to take / have a leisurely bath.（悠閒地泡個澡真是令人神清氣爽），而其中的 leisurely 就是「悠閒地；從容不迫地」之意。另，洗「戰鬥澡；快速地洗澡」則説成 have a quick bath。

19 我今晚不想泡澡。也許明早再泡吧。
I don't feel like taking a bath tonight. Maybe I'll take one in the morning.

20 這個面膜讓我覺得彷彿置身美容沙龍。
This facial mask makes me feel like I'm at a beauty salon.

21 沒有什麼比沐浴後的一杯啤酒更美味的了。
Nothing tastes better than a beer after a bath.

22 我想我會喝杯睡前酒。
I think I will have a nightcap.

23 在我打盹的同時，電視就這樣播完了。
Broadcasting on TV finished while I was dozing off.

24 我最近都沒打電話回家給父母。
I haven't phoned home to my parents recently.

not feel like ~ = 不想~ cf. be reluctant to ~ = 不情願做~

此例中第 2 句的 one 就是指 a bath。而「沖澡；淋浴」説成 take a shower，「早上洗頭」則是 <u>wash</u> / <u>shampoo</u> one's hair in the morning。

---

facial mask = 面膜／make ~ feel like … = 讓~覺得像……／beauty salon (= aesthetic <u>salon</u>/<u>spa</u>) = 美容院；美容沙龍

「接受美容護理服務」説成 <u>get</u> / <u>receive</u> beauty <u>salon</u> / <u>spa</u> treatment。

Nothing ~ better than … = 沒有什麼~比……更棒了／taste = 嚐起來／a beer = 一杯／一瓶啤酒

此例句也可説成 A beer after a bath is so good.。而「我沐浴後總會喝上一杯啤酒」就説成 I always have a beer after my bath.。

---

nightcap = 睡前酒／<u>have</u>/<u>take</u> a nightcap = 喝睡前酒

「在睡前喝一杯」説成 have a drink <u>before bed</u> / <u>at bedtime</u>，而「喝杯睡前酒如何？」就説成 How about a nightcap?。

---

broadcasting on TV = 電視節目的播放／while ~ = 在~的同時／doze off (= nod off) = 打盹；打瞌睡／nap = 小睡

「電視收播後的雜訊」可用 snow noise 或 "snowy" noise pattern 來表達。

---

phone (= call) = 打電話

此例句也可説成 I haven't called my parents.。「老家」就是 one's parents home（父母親的家）。「回老家」可説成 go home to [see] one's parents。

25 我每天就只是往返於工作與家中。我的人生僅止於此了嗎？

Every day I just go back and forth to work. Is this all there is to my life?

26 人生不會總是一帆風順。

Things don't always go well in life.

27 我必須訂定計畫，為明天做好準備。

I have to work out a plan and make arrangements for tomorrow.

28 一想到明天的會議，我就很鬱卒。

I feel down when I think about the meeting tomorrow.

29 我要去睡了。多想也沒用。

I'll go to bed now. It's no use thinking about it.

30 睡前我得確認門都已經鎖好了。

I have to make sure the doors are locked before going to bed.

go back and forth = 往返；來回 cf. back and forth = 來來回回地；往返地（注意，中文的「往返」兩字與英文剛好顛倒）／go to and from = 往返／That is all there is = 僅止於此

此例的第 2 句也可説成 Is this life all right for me?（這樣的人生對我來説好嗎？）。

---

go well = 順利 e.g. Things went well. = 事情進展順利／If everything goes well = 若一切順利

「這就是人生」説成 That's life.，「人生充滿了高低起伏」則説成 Life is full of ups and downs.。

---

work out a plan = 訂定計畫／make arrangements for ～ = 為～做準備；安排 ～

也可將此例前半句 I have to work out a plan ... 中的 plan 做為動詞使用，説成 I have to plan ...。

---

feel down (= feel low) = 情緒低落 cf. get / become depressed = 變得沮喪

cheer oneself up 就是「激勵自我；替自己打氣」的意思，而要激勵別人、表達「振作點！」之意時，則用 Cheer up!

---

go to bed = 上床睡覺；就寢／It's no use -ing = ～是沒有用的

此例的第 2 句也可説成 It's useless thinking about it.。而「過度擔心」説成 worry too much，要別人「放輕鬆！」則可説 Take it easy!

---

make sure = 確認；確定

「關窗」説成 shut / close a window。「防盜警報器；防盜警鈴」是 burglar alarm；「住家保全系統」是 home security system；「保全公司」則是 security company / firm。

31 我要把鬧鐘設成 7 點。
I'll set the alarm clock for seven [o'clock].

32 今晚我一上床便會立刻睡著。
Tonight I'll fall asleep as soon as my head hits the pillow.

33 我晾了墊被，所以它恢復了蓬鬆而且有清新的陽光氣味。
I aired out my futon, so it's puffed up again and smells like fresh sunshine.

34 天氣很冷，我也許該再加一條毯子。
It's chilly, so maybe I should put on another blanket.

35 我做了惡夢。我睡出一身冷汗。
I had a bad dream. I sweat a lot in my sleep.

36 這些孩子真的很好睡。
The kids got to sleep so easily.

set the alarm clock for ~ [o'clock] = 把鬧鐘設成～點

「鬧鐘響起」說成 alarm clock goes off，而「被鬧鐘叫醒」則說成 wake up to an alarm clock。

---

fall asleep = 睡著／pillow = 枕頭

此例句直譯成中文就是「頭碰到枕頭的瞬間，便會睡著」。而「熟睡」可說成 sleep soundly 或 sleep like a log / top。此外，在睡前可對別人說 Sleep tight! 「睡個好覺！」。

---

air out futon = 晾曬墊被 cf. hang futon [up] outside = 把墊被掛在外面曬／puff up = 使～蓬鬆／smell like ~ = 有～的氣味／fresh = 新鮮的；清新的

此例的前半句也可說成 I hung my futon outside, so ...（我把墊被掛在外面曬，所以⋯⋯）。

---

chilly =寒冷的；冷颼颼的 cf. cold = 冷的／put on ~ = 穿上～；披上～／blanket = 毯子 cf. electric[al] blanket = 電毯／comforter = 蓋被；棉被／summer quilt = 夏天的涼被／duvet = 羽絨被

---

bad dream (= nightmare) = 惡夢／sweat a lot = 流了很多汗／in my sleep = 在我睡覺時 e.g. I talk in my sleep. = 我說夢話

此例的第 2 句也可說成 I had night sweats.「我在夜間盜汗」。

---

get to sleep = 睡著；入睡 cf. can't get to sleep = 睡不著

此例句也可說成 The kids fell asleep really quickly.。而「早睡早起」就是 early to bed and early to rise。另外，「早起型的人」則說成 morning person。

37 再上一天班就是週末了！

One more day at the office, then it's the weekend!

38 明天開始就是週末連假啦！萬歲！

The long weekend starts tomorrow! Hurray!

39 我明天也會全力以赴！

I'll do my best tomorrow, too!

one more day = 再一天／at the office = 在辦公室

one more day to go 是「只要再過一天」之意。而「感謝老天，終於到週五了！」說成 Thank God it's Friday!（可縮寫成 TGIF）。

---

long weekend = 較長的週末連假（例如週一是國定假日）cf. three-day weekend = 連放三天的週末假期／holidays in a row = 連續假期／Hurray/Hurrah! = 萬歲！；耶！

注意，Bravo! 是針對進行順利的事情所發出的喝采、稱讚聲，並不適合用在此處。

---

do one's best = 全力以赴

要激勵、鼓勵人的話，可用 Hang on!（撐下去）、Go for it!（朝目標邁進）、Keep it up!（繼續努力）、Give it your best!（全力衝刺）等說法來表達。

Skit  夜晚篇

連假前夜的短暫喘息

Woman: **Are the kids asleep❶?**

Man: **Yes. I was going to read a bedtime story to them but they fell asleep really quickly.**

W: **Great! Now we can relax❷. How about❸ a bath? It's so refreshing to take a leisurely bath.**

M: **We've both been working too hard. I'll heat up the bath water.**

W: **Use a good bath powder as a reward. I'm going to shampoo my hair and shave my legs.**

M: **I want to take off my tie and hang up my jacket first. Business suits are so uncomfortable.**

W: **Well, one more day at the office, then it's the weekend.**

M: **That's right! The long weekend starts tomorrow! Hurray!**

W: **Don't get too excited. We have to take Jason to soccer practice❹ and take Bailey to her karate class, buy shoes for Jason, get a birthday present for Bailey, and make sure❺ both kids have all the school supplies❻ they need.**

M: **Man❼, life with kids isn't easy.**

W: **Maybe we could trade them in for❽ a pet dog!**

女子：孩子們都睡著了嗎？

男子：是啊。我本來想唸睡前床邊故事哄他們睡的，但是他們很快就睡著了。

女：太好了！現在我們可以放輕鬆了。泡個澡如何？悠閒地泡個澡會令人神清氣爽。

男：我們兩個都太努力工作了。我來熱洗澡水。

女：用好的泡澡粉當作對自己的獎勵吧。我要洗個頭，還要剃一下腿毛。

男：我要先把領帶拿掉、把外套掛好。穿西裝真是不舒服。

女：嗯，再上一天班就是週末了！

男：沒錯！明天開始就是週末連假啦！萬歲！

女：別太高興了。我們得帶傑森去參加足球的練習、帶貝莉去上她的空手道課、替傑森買鞋、替貝莉買生日禮物，還要確保兩個小鬼需要的學校用品都備齊了才行。

男：啊，有小孩的生活可真不輕鬆。

女：也許我們可以拿小孩換隻寵物狗回來！

【單字片語】

❶ asleep：睡著的

❷ relax：休息；放鬆

❸ How about ~?：做～如何？

❹ soccer practice：足球的練習

❺ make sure ~：確保～

❻ school supplies：學校用品（supplies 是指「必需品」）

❼ Man：啊（感嘆詞，用來表示驚訝、無奈、氣憤等）

❽ trade A in for B：拿 A 來換取 B

Quick Check

讓我們一起來複習本章所介紹過的句型！請依據以下中文句子的意思，來完成對應的英文句子。（答案就在本頁最下方。）

❶ 我預先準備明天的晚餐。→P253

I ( ) ( ) ( ) for tomorrow's dinner.

❷ 我妥善照顧我的身體。→P255

I ( ) ( ) ( ) ( ) my body.

❸ 我熬夜。→P256

I ( ) ( ) ( ).

❹ 我上床〔準備睡覺〕。→P256

I ( ) ( ) ( ).

❺ 我會用微波爐把這個加熱當晚餐吃。→P260

I'll ( ) this ( ) my dinner.

❻ 我今晚不想泡澡。也許明早再泡吧。→P264

I don't ( ) ( ) ( ) ( ) ( ) tonight.
Maybe I'll ( ) ( ) in the morning.

❼ 沒有什麼比沐浴後的一杯啤酒更美味的了。→P264

( ) ( ) ( ) ( ) a beer after a bath.

❽ 我必須訂定計畫，為明天做好準備。→P266

I have to ( ) ( ) a plan and ( ) ( ) for tomorrow.

❾ 今晚我一上床便會立刻睡著。→P268

Tonight ( ) ( ) ( ) as soon as my head ( ) ( ) ( ).

❿ 我明天也會全力以赴！→P270

I'll ( ) ( ) ( ) tomorrow, too!

---

❶ prepare/in/advance ❷ take/good/care/of
❸ stay/up/late ❹ get/into/bed ❺ microwave/
for ❻ feel/like/taking/a/bath/take/one ❼

Nothing/tastes/better/than ❽ work/out/
make/arrangements ❾ I'll/fall/asleep/hits/
the/pillow ❿ do/my/best

國家圖書館出版品預行編目資料

神明護體學英文—日常英語篇 / 吉田研作, 荒井貴和, 武藤克彦　作；
陳亦苓翻譯. -- 初版. -- 臺北市：貝塔, 2012. 06
　　面：　　公分

　ISBN: 978-957-729-892-8（平裝）

　1. 英語　2. 會話

805.188
101011233

神明護體學英文—日常英語篇

作　　者 / 吉田研作、荒井貴和、武藤克彦
總 編 審 / 王復國
翻　　譯 / 陳亦苓
執行編輯 / 朱慧瑛

出　　版 / 貝塔出版有限公司
地　　址 / 100 台北市館前路 12 號 11 樓
電　　話 / (02) 2314-2525
傳　　真 / (02) 2312-3535
郵　　撥 / 19493777 貝塔出版有限公司
客服專線 / (02) 2314-3535
客服信箱 / btservice@betamedia.com.tw

總 經 銷 / 時報文化出版企業股份有限公司
地　　址 / 桃園縣龜山鄉萬壽路二段 351 號
電　　話 / (02) 2306-6842

出版日期 / 2012 年 8 月初版一刷
定　　價 / 320 元
I S B N / 978-957-729-892-8

「完全改訂版　起きてから寝るまで英語表現700」
　吉田研作、荒井貴和、武藤克彦　著

"KANZEN KAITEIBAN OKITEKARA NERUMADE EIGO HYOGEN 700"
by Kensaku Yoshida, Kiwa Arai, Katsuhiko Muto
Copyright © Kensaku Yoshida, Kiwa Arai, Katsuhiko Muto, ALC Press, Inc. 2010
All rights reserved.
Original Japanese edition published by ALC Press, Inc.
This edition is published by arrangement with ALC Press, Inc., Tokyo
through Tuttle-Mori Agency, Inc., Tokyo and Keio Cultural Enterprise Co., Ltd.,
New Taipei City
貝塔網址：www.betamedia.com.tw

喚醒你的英文語感 ！

請對折後釘好，直接寄回即可！

| 廣　告　回　信 |
| 北區郵政管理局登記證 |
| 北台字第14256號 |
| 免　貼　郵　票 |

100 台北市中正區館前路12號11樓

 貝塔語言出版 收
Beta Multimedia Publishing

寄件者住址 □□□

謝謝您購買本書！！

貝塔語言擁有最優良之英文學習書籍，為提供您最佳的英語學習資訊，您可填妥此表後寄回（免貼郵票）將可不定期收到本公司最新發行書訊及活動訊息！

姓名：_____　性別：□男 □女　生日：____年____月____日

電話：(公)_____ (宅)_____ (手機)_____

電子信箱：_____

學歷：□高中職含以下　□專科　□大學　□研究所含以上

職業：□金融　□服務　□傳播　□製造　□資訊　□軍公教　□出版

　　　□自由　□教育　□學生　□其他

職級：□企業負責人　□高階主管　□中階主管　□職員　□專業人士

1. 您購買的書籍是？_____

2. 您從何處得知本產品？(可複選)

　　　□書店 □網路 □書展 □校園活動 □廣告信函 □他人推薦 □新聞報導 □其他

3. 您覺得本產品價格：

　　　□偏高 □合理 □偏低

4. 請問目前您每週花了多少時間學英語？

　　　□ 不到十分鐘 □ 十分鐘以上，但不到半小時 □ 半小時以上，但不到一小時

　　　□ 一小時以上，但不到兩小時 □ 兩個小時以上 □ 不一定

5. 通常在選擇語言學習書時，哪些因素是您會考慮的？

　　　□ 封面 □ 內容、實用性 □ 品牌 □ 媒體、朋友推薦 □ 價格 □ 其他_____

6. 市面上您最需要的語言書種類為？

　　　□ 聽力 □ 閱讀 □ 文法 □ 口說 □ 寫作 □ 其他_____

7. 通常您會透過何種方式選購語言學習書籍？

　　　□ 書店門市 □ 網路書店 □ 郵購 □ 直接找出版社 □ 學校或公司團購

　　　□ 其他_____

8. 給我們的建議：_____

_____

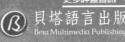